*Tales
from
Academy
Street*

Tales from Academy Street

Martha Derman

SCHOLASTIC
HARDCOVER

Scholastic Inc.
New York

Library of Congress Cataloging-in-Publication Data

Derman, Martha.
    Tales from Academy Street / Martha Derman.
        p.   cm.
    Summary: A collection of stories in which mysterious, spooky, and funny things happen to the kids who live on Academy Street.

ISBN 0-590-43703-8

    [1. Supernatural—Fiction.]   I. Title.
PZ7.D444Tal   1991
[Fic]—dc20   90-23363
                                                                   CIP
                                                                    AC

12 11 10 9 8 7 6 5 4 3 2 1   1 2 3 4 5 6/9

                        Printed in the U.S.A.   37

                First Scholastic printing, September 1991

This one
is for
Adam

On Academy Street:
After Labor Day

DUCHESS, THE RUMPLED YELLOW RETRIEVER
from the Gilderslieve house, trotted down Academy
Street, stopping near the corner at Pond Road to
sniff at a big drainage pipe. She whined and
scratched, then poked her head inside. The pipe had
a permanent resident, never seen by anyone who
lived on Academy Street. He was an enormous toad,
round as Duchess's feeding bowl and camouflaged
in the colors of an army tank.

When Duchess could not find him, she walked to
the corner. It was the opening day of school, and
this year, as she had for the past five years, Duchess
settled down by the street post, ready for the return

1

of the ten children who always got off at Academy Street.

Promptly at 3:18 the bus was due. Mothers took jobs and hired baby-sitters based on the regularity of school buses. Life was like that in Thorne Center. Families lived nice and easy in the midst of narrow green lawns and under the arch of oaks and maples. One day was much like the next.

But this afternoon a chilly wind ruffled the fur along Duchess's back. Clouds built up over the road, great boiling thunderheads. For sure it was hurricane weather, and Duchess stood up, aware of electricity in the air. There, lightning flashed. Duchess sniffed and whined and shifted the position of her paws. The wind whipped at her ears, and fat water drops bounced in the dust around her. She ought to run home, but what would the kids do without her to meet the bus?

Duchess held firm even as slashes of icy hail began to beat into the bushes and along her ribs. *Urrrg.* She blinked, sneezed, and cowered. A hailstone landed over her right eye and stung. She galloped to the drainage pipe and squeezed inside as far as she could go.

Down the road, the bus slugged along. Hail-stones, the size of hickory nuts, plinkplunked against the roof, blown by the wildness of the weather. The boys and girls who lined the aisle to get off at Academy Street hesitated when the door hissed open. "Sorry, kids," said the driver. "It's only a little hail to celebrate school starting. Ha-ha! Let's go. Out!"

Whooping, they each took the plunge into the storm. Adrienne Gilderslieve paused on the bus steps to yell to Beth, "Come over when it stops, Beth."

Linda Hillyer, next off, listened to the wheezing wind and *sh-sh-ing* of the hail. She half liked frightening herself by imagining voices in the wind. Linda held her notebook over her head and ran. She passed Adrienne, who laughed and twirled in the hail, arms outstretched. Adrienne was one grade behind Linda, and everyone knew she was kind of far-out.

A knot of boys hustled out to skid and slide along the hill. Streak Baxter, from junior high, raced ahead. He usually won even though the Pennell twins were bigger. "Hey, wait up!" shouted one of them, Jeff or maybe Chris. It did not seem to make any difference how fast anyone ran; the hail hit each one equally.

Duchess, muddy tail waving, backed out of the drainage pipe to join Adrienne and her sisters, Meaghan and Nora.

"Cuckoo dog doesn't know enough to stay home out of the rain," said Nora.

"Bad as Adrienne," said Meaghan scornfully. Adrienne had Duchess by the forepaws and was dancing her around in the wet.

"*Yip-yippety*," barked Duchess.

No one observed Jesse Kujak fall into step with Liz Pennell and wrap his blue jacket around her shoulders. Jesse was the oldest boy on the street, different because he was deaf.

Draped with denim, Liz walked beside Jesse. She said, "Uh, thanks," about the jacket. It felt too heavy over her dampened sweatshirt, but she pretended to like it. She hoped Adrienne would not notice Jesse's gesture because Adrienne would hoot. Then everybody, including Cara Nerone, would notice. The other girls thought Jesse was such a loser that Liz hated to admit she really liked him. She drew the jacket collar up to her ears and smiled at Jesse. He had speckles of ice clinging to his eyebrows.

Not tall, but broad-shouldered, with a tumble of untamed hair that was also collecting bits of ice, Jesse wore a pink squiggle of a hearing aid in one ear. Liz wondered if all the wet would hurt it. As thunder boomed overhead, she tried to imagine how it sounded to Jesse.

Liz thought about things like that. Jesse had great appeal to her imagination. He was supposed to be some kind of an artistic genius at school. Everyone knew he took special art classes and graphics design. That gave him a standout reputation. It was too easy, Liz felt, for other kids to forget that as they listened to Jesse's "What-what?" whenever he lost track of the general conversation. They ought to realize he depended on lip-reading to help him separate the sounds filtered through the hearing aid. It was like learning another language.

"Lip-reading," Liz mouthed silently into the wind and moved her lips around each syllable.

"What?" said Jesse. Oops, he thought she'd said something.

Liz yelled over the weather, "Nothing, Jesse." They paused at Liz's front walk. Liz knew her hair was plastered to her forehead; she must look a wreck. Still, she took time to speak so he could watch her mouth. "Here's your jacket, thanks a lot. I'll go in now."

Drops sliding from his chin, though the storm was letting up, Jesse said, "You want to come up this afternoon? I can show you how to paint a T-shirt."

"Maybe later. *Later*, I said." Sometimes you had an urge to screech at the top of your lungs to make Jesse understand. She did not want to hurt his feelings, but it was hard always to remember he needed a little special attention.

Jesse said, "Okay," swung his jacket over one shoulder, and strode up the hill toward his house. The storm was already slackening as he walked.

As Jesse passed the Nerones' mailbox, Cara was slipping its contents into her school pack to keep the mail dry. Knowing that Jesse would not hear her, she called down to Liz, "Honestly, what did *he* want?"

Irked at what was none of Cara's business, Liz pushed her wet hair back and answered, "Nothing much."

Cara laughed an insulting laugh. "Just being *friendly*, I suppose."

Liz ignored the emphasis on "friendly." "Sure," she said and changed the subject. "Hey, the rain's stopped."

"Crazy weather," said Cara. "Want to come over?"

Liz examined the sky where the clouds were breaking. "Maybe," she said. She was not going to tell Cara she was going to Jesse's. No way. "After a while," she murmured. Strange how she felt as changeable as the day, liking, disliking Cara from one minute to the next.

Now the sun glared down between a rift in the clouds, and steam rose from rivulets of melted hail. The pavement let go twists of mist fit to decorate a Frankenstein castle.

Running back and forth through the wet, Duchess escorted the three Gilderslieve sisters toward their house. She had a little trouble getting Adrienne inside. Meaghan and Nora hurried in, but Duchess had to grab Adrienne by her plaid skirt and pull her toward the door. "Go chase a bone, you dippy dog," yelled Adrienne. "The sun's out."

As quickly as the sun had shone, a blue-black cloud obscured it. Lightning seemed to roll out of the sky in a sheet of electricity, and a thunderclap crashed over their heads, *Boom-kaboom.*

"I'm coming," hollered Adrienne. "Hold the door." Close on Adrienne's heels, Duchess pushed her into safety. From ears to tail, she shook water from her fur all over Nora.

"Thanks a lot," said Nora.

"Way to go," said Adrienne. "Good dog."

THAT AFTERNOON:
Jesse's Feet

JESSE ENTERED THE KUJAK HOUSE BY THE basement door. He shook the water out of his hair much like Duchess shaking her fur. He stamped his feet clear of slush. He was proud of his own room in the basement, and he did not want to track in the wet. All his stuff was there: his paints and a tall drawing table, his stereo and his books. He also had a set of barbells in one corner.

He could not hear his mother scrape a chair over the floor upstairs, but she heard him switch on his stereo. That was one of the reasons he had this downstairs pad. He played music so loud, his mother said she'd get as deaf as he was.

Jesse left the door to his room open, so his tape

echoed around the basement. Sound was more reassuring than quiet. He climbed the stairs to a door
that led into the kitchen and opened it. "Hi, Ma,"
he said.

Mrs. Kujak sat at the kitchen table. She looked up
and smiled. "Hello, Jess. Are you wet from that sud-
den storm?"

"Only damp," said Jesse. "Didn't last. Anything
to eat?" Jesse swung the refrigerator door wide to
check what was on the shelves.

"I have to shop for more this afternoon," his
mother said loudly. "Let me tell you what's left there
before you let all the cold out." Jesse closed the door
and sat down to watch his mother's lips.

"Smoked turkey. Apples in fruit drawer. Bread's
in the freezer, sliced. You have to toast it."

"Okay, thanks."

"I bought you something this morning. They had
a sale at Cashncarry Shoes. These are your size." His
mother pushed a bag toward him. "Take off those
wet sneakers and try these."

Jesse opened the bag and pulled out a pair of
sneakers, big as boats they seemed, because they were
gleaming white, toe to heel. "Ma, they're so *clean*."

"I should hope so, dear. Throw those disgusting
dirty things you're wearing in the trash."

"I'll take a san'ich downstairs and try the shoes,"
Jesse said.

"Jesse. Look at me. San*d*-wich. Say it."

9

"Yeah. Sand-wich. I forgot."

After his mother had driven their old station wagon to the supermarket, Jesse sat on the shabby couch in his room and bit into his turkey on toasted rye. "Sand-wich," he muttered through mayonnaise. Then he put the bread down. He stripped off his sweater and flexed his shoulders. Best to warm up with the bars a little just to get limber. Exercise first, and the sand-wich would taste better afterwards.

After a tense day at school, it felt good to break out a sweat. Being hard of hearing the way he was, he had to concentrate so hard on lessons, he could raise a headache in some classes without half trying. Pumping iron cleared his head and smoothed the knots out of his stomach.

Jesse squatted, then stood erect. He lifted the barbell up and pushed it over his head. "Uhnnn." He did it three times, then lowered the bar in stages to the floor. Enough for now. He shoved it toward its corner with his foot.

Jesse frowned at the foot, at both feet. He sat down with his sand-wich and thought while he ate. His mother just did not understand how sneakers were at school. There, it was impossible ever to admit you had *new* sneakers. When you were a little kid in the lower grades, you could wear clean new Adidas or Reeboks or whatever. Big kids like him were just supposed to *have* sneakers, gray and scuffed. It was as if you were born with 'em or something. Show

up in stuff like these, and people'd make jokes he
wouldn't hear the whole day. He'd have to say
"What-what?" and that was so dumb. He'd better
give the jerks something to holler about, so he could
just grin, and let the sneaks, kind of, speak for
themselves.

He chuckled to himself, hardly aware any longer
how his chuckle sounded through his hearing aid.
Rumble-rumble, mostly. He took a jar stuck full of
Day-Glo markers from a shelf. He kicked off his old
sneakers and wiggled his toes.

Now, he'd fix those new ones.

He sat on his couch and scooped the sneakers from
the floor. He turned them onto his knees. "Made in
Yugoslavia" was printed across the center of the
white rubber sole. He had never managed geography
too well, and he wondered where Yugoslavia was.

No matter. Jesse selected a purple marker and set
to work. Almost without thinking he drew an eyeball
on the toe of his left sneaker. He colored the pupil
black and striped the iris green and blue. He held
the sneaker over his head so he could view the eye,
a rather Egyptian pharaoh's ellipse, upside down.
Good poster effect! He drew a matching eye on the
right.

As he glanced at the left shoe to check if the eye
matched its mate, he thought he caught the pupil
moving to look at the eye on the right. Impossible!
He repeated his movements and glanced again.

Nothing happened. That had been an illusion. "Ill-oo-shun," he mouthed to remind himself.

Out of the corners of his own eyes, he got the impression that the lid of the right eye lowered and then raised, like a wink. Jesse's hand jerked in surprise. Cut it out, Jesse told himself, but he had scrawled an unplanned zigzag before he realized it. "Geez," he said aloud. His hearing aid squeaked.

He rubbed his ear, then checked the outlined eyes again. They stared up at him as blank as drawn eyes usually seemed.

But now all that Jesse saw was that mistake, that scrawled zigzag. He had to turn it into a pattern on both shoes. He stared at the wall; what to make of it? He remembered once seeing wings on some museum lions. So how about wings? he thought, and completed the zigzag as a pair of wings on each foot. He outlined them with purple, and feathered them in red and yellow.

Great! If he squinted at them, he could almost see the wings fluttering.

Each sneaker had come with new laces, wrapped in a strip of silver paper, shoved into the toe. Jesse tipped the shoes to let the laces fall onto the couch. The tongues, spandy clean, hung out like a panting dog's. Hey, crrrazy! Jesse had a notion to color them Day-Glo red.

He crosshatched each tongue with red and orange. The colors would show up perfect through the white

12

laces. "Needs a mouth," he said. "Both of 'em." His hearing aid echoed in its friendly fashion. Jesse selected a strident pink and, across the brass eyelets, extending from his instep to the opposite side, he drew wide lips.

"Awesome," Jesse said. He spoke aloud, but his aid was very silent.

"Dare you wear us?" he imagined a voice asking.

He inserted the laces loosely in each sneaker and placed the two on the floor so he could slip his feet in. When he tied the laces, his hearing aid went into a tailspin of crackles. Probably needed a new battery. In a minute. He detached the plastic from his ear and put it in his pocket.

Jesse stood up to admire his feet. Static zapped through his ear, and he heard shrill voices. He automatically put up a finger to adjust the volume control on his aid, but of course, he'd already removed the earpiece.

What *was* this? There was no one there, just him. "Who's talking?" he asked and checked his stereo. It was off — the end of the tape.

He paced back and forth, knowing it was stupid to think there was a place for anyone to hide. For some reason he kept stumbling over nothing. Probably the fault of the new sneakers. They were so stiff they seemed to have a will of their own. He got down to poke under the couch. Nothing, except he thought he heard a burst of giggles. He stood so that he could put his hand in his pocket to be sure. Yup, that was where his aid was. How come he was hearing stuff?

Oops! He almost lost his balance and had to sit down on his couch in a hurry. "Hey, quit foolin' around!" he shouted, then felt real dumb. Who did he suppose he was talking to?

Jesse planted his feet deliberately on the floor. He wished the static in his ears would calm down. He'd never had this problem before, hearing voices that kind of crooned together, "Out . . . out . . . owowout!"

He clamped his palms over his ears, but he still heard voices calling shrilly. "Listen," he said, sweating slightly, "who are you? Where are you?" It was best, sometimes, to tough things out. "S-speak up."

"Right here," said two thin disturbing voices from below his knees.

"Milan," said a single voice from floor level.

"Andrej," said another from beside the first.

Jesse jerked both feet off the floor. "You!" he said, "you, shoes?"

"What did you give us wings for? We want to fly ho-o-ome!" In the new sneakers, Jesse's feet kept trying to rise from the floor.

Jesse stiffened his toes and heels to stop such nonsense. Even though his heart was beating a mile a minute, he said, "This *is* home," to the sneakers.

"Not ours," asserted the doubled voice. He heard

14

too distinctly without his aid. And that was impossible, too. His aid gave him the sounds of the real world.

Jesse kicked off the sneakers and hoped they'd shut up. Instead, the empty sneakers acted, he thought, like Mexican jumping beans he'd seen once. They skittered in circles. He leaned down to pick up the nearest, but it hopped away. There were more high-pitched giggles.

"Wait a mo', Jess," he told himself. "Play it cool, man." He swallowed. "Where is your home, you guys?"

They answered in unison, "The great nation of Zagreb, Ljubliana, Beograd . . ."

"How do I know where they are?"

"Yu-go-sla-via!"

"Then how come you speak such good English?"

But when they answered this time, he could not understand a word. He supposed they answered in whatever Yugoslav people spoke.

Jesse narrowed his eyes and lifted his chin. What would happen to his talky shoes if he put his aid in his ear? His hearing aid brought him all the ordinary sounds he needed. Fact is, he could not call these voices anything except, well, *extra*-ordinary.

From a drawer he removed a small plastic case and shook a wafer of a battery into his palm. He exchanged the old battery for the new one and lifted a lock of hair to fit the squiggle of aid into his ear.

He fiddled a little with the volume control, but there was not a sound in his room to guide him.

Jesse kicked at the nearest sneaker to make it talk. It didn't. He threw his sweater over the second one to see if it would holler for air. There was no muffled cry for help. He removed the aid he had just placed in his ear.

"BRRRZAP!" The crosshatched tongues blew a Bronx cheer. How'd they learn that in Yugoslavia?

"Fix you good," Jesse said and pushed his aid firmly into his ear. Utter silence.

Jesse gathered up the sneakers and sat down with them in his lap. He still liked the way he had drawn designs upon them. The brilliant colors in the eyes and the wings really spoke to him. Well, no, not *spoke* exactly, but the decorations deeply pleased him. If he was going to wear them, he must rely on his aid as, after all, he always did, to keep the shoes silent. He knew people often took him for an oddball, and he did not need something as weird as talking sneakers to put kids off any more than usual.

A firm knocking came from his door. He heard it clearly through his aid. Who besides his parents knew how to come through the garage to his inner room?

He opened the door and grinned with real pleasure. It was Liz, holding up a white cotton shirt. "Do you have time to paint T-shirts now? Oh!" She noticed the sneakers that Jesse had placed on his couch. "They're gorgeous."

"You like them?" said Jesse. "I was just going to put them on." He gritted his teeth. That was exactly what he was going to do, too. He sat down and stuck his socks feetfirst into Milan and then into Andrej.

Silence. Jesse patted his hearing aid.

Liz was talking, but he had not concentrated on her voice. "What-what?" Jesse said. He was so glad to see her, real and freckled and blue-eyed as she was.

"Original," Liz said as she faced him. "They are so original, your sneakers."

Jesse tied double knots in the laces. There was not a hint of protest. "Yeah," he said. "I thought maybe I overdid it — the Egyptian eyes, the wings, the big mouths . . . too freaky for most guys."

"I like things freaky the way you do them," said Liz. "Can I draw wings on my T-shirt?"

Jesse fingered the label on the shirt. "Made in Hong Kong," it said. If he took his hearing aid out of his ear, would the shirt speak to him about flying home? Huh, he was not about to try it. "No Hong Kong flights," he whispered to himself.

"What?" said Liz.

Grinning, Jesse mimicked himself. "What-what?" Truth was, with Liz to watch him he felt strong enough to hear anything.

17

LATE SEPTEMBER:
Mr. Chop

THE HILLYERS LIVED IN A SMALL GRAY HOUSE near the first rise of the Academy Street hill. Linda Hillyer, mousey blonde hair and gray eyes, was younger than Cara and Liz, but older than Adrienne Gilders. That way it worked out that she did not have a real close neighborhood friend. She did not feel lonely though, because everyone on the street was friendly.

Maybe because there wasn't anyone her exact age living near, or because it was just how Linda was, she was especially curious about anybody new. She would have been very interested in the late September day when Mr. Chop discovered Academy Street. She would have noticed immediately his old-fashioned clothes and puzzled over the way he hovered over the the tiny pond at the foot of her street. Once he had parked his rusty black bicycle against some bushes, she would have wondered why he patted the surface of the water.

But as it happened, Linda did not see Mr. Chop until she went to collect her family's mail from the mailbox at the end of her driveway. Then she saw Mr. Chop pumping his bike up the hill. Wire saddlebags rattled on the rear wheel, and a rake and a hoe poked up their long handles. She had time to notice that he wore a velvety corduroy suit and his calves were wrapped in bright yellow leggings. They were like the gaiters cross-country skiers wear, or even the old-fashioned skaters on Christmas cards. Neat clothes, Linda thought, not like her father's dull gray flannel suit.

Near Linda the man stopped and doffed his soft green hat. He had smooth dark hair and wore a very white kerchief knotted about his throat. Linda felt flattered to have a hat taken off to *her*, as if she were a grown-up.

"Good day," the man said. "This house need a gardener?"

"I don't think so," said Linda, but his smile was so warm that it made her wish she could say "sure."

"The mother or father home?"

"My mother is home this afternoon."

"Give her the card. I look around and prepare to

19

talk with her." His speech seemed formal and odd to Linda, but pleasing and very friendly. He made her feel important.

The man fumbled at a pocket in his dark brown vest, a rich chestnut brown in contrast to his tan corduroys, and drew out a small business card. "Pronounce 'Chop.'" The man's index finger pointed to the center of the card where Linda read: M. Czap, Lawn Tree and Garden Care. Telephone — 555-5273. She admired the printing of little blue feathers around the edges of the card. Pretty.

"C-Z-A-P, Chop," the man repeated.

Linda took the card into the house. "Mom, a man wants to talk to you about gardening."

"Tell him we don't need a gardener."

"I think you ought to see how he's dressed, Mom." Linda thrust the feather-decorated card at Mrs. Hillyer. "He's, well, I guess maybe, he's distinguished-looking, even on an old black bike."

Her mother went outside. Linda peeked from a kitchen window. She saw Mr. Chop lean his bicycle against the hedge and again remove his sporty hat. Linda had a chapter due for English so she settled into her favorite chair to read. But when her mother returned, Linda had to ask, "What did you tell him?"

"I said he could come on the weekend and talk to your father. He *is* sweet and so polite, isn't he?"

After dinner, Mrs. Hillyer mentioned to Linda's father that she had talked with a gardener who wanted to make the yard ready for winter.

"See here, gardeners are too expensive. We can't afford him."

"You tell him," said Mrs. Hillyer. "He's coming on Saturday, I think."

"You don't know how to be firm with people," said Linda's father.

At dawn on Saturday, before anyone even thought of getting up, the Hillyers were jarred awake by a raucous clatter on the lawn below the bedroom window. Linda moaned to herself and turned over to see her clock. It was only six A.M. Her tiger tabby, Muffy, who slept at her feet, opened one eye.

Linda heard her father bang down the stairs and yell out the dining room windows. The gabbling continued. In minutes she heard him stomp back upstairs and called out, "What is it, Daddy?"

"Damn ducks eating crab apples."

"Who has ducks around here?"

"Nobody. These are wild ducks. Mallards. Where's the cat? She'll chase 'em away." Her father grabbed Muffy and descended with the cat yawning under one arm.

Added to the hoarse chattering below came a flapping, beating, and rapid fluttering of wings. Even Linda's windows seemed to rattle. Then, there was a long, drawn-out howl, Muffy at her unhappiest. In a moment the cat bounded into Linda's room, ears laid back, tail fluffed out giant-size, to hide un-

21

der the bed. "What happened?" Linda sat up. She was wide awake now.

Her father stood in her doorway. "Cowardly cat," he said, "and too many determined ducks. You could say that old Muffy has been duck-pecked."

While they were eating breakfast, Mr. Chop, in his green hat, red-brown vest, and corduroys, rode his bicycle onto the lawn. When he turned, they saw a blue bandanna dangled from a rear pocket. "That your Mr. Chop?" said Linda's father. "Odd sort of duck."

"Well, honestly, Ed. I thought he was quite nice."

"Me, too," said Linda.

She watched her father go out to meet Mr. Chop. She hoped he would not be harsh toward that gardener. She saw that he and Mr. Chop walked around the two crab apple trees.

"Everything settled?" said Mrs. Hillyer when Linda's father reappeared a half hour later. "You got rid of him?"

"Uh, he's working for half price this fall."

Inside her chest, Linda's heart gave a little lurch of what might have been joy.

"I see. Can he get rid of the ducks, did you ask?"

"He said crab apples are very nourishing, but he'd make sure the ducks were quiet hereafter."

"How is he going to do *that*?"

Mr. Hillyer rubbed his hands up and down his cheeks, *scritch-scritch*, because he had not shaved yet.

"Funny thing, at the time it seemed okay. I think he said he'd speak to them. That can't be right. He probably said something about he'd *keep* the ducks away, I think."

"Edward!" Mrs. Hillyer glanced at Linda, and she and Linda laughed.

"*I* think we're hooked on Mr. Chop," said Mrs. Hillyer.

Although there had never been ducks on the Academy Street pond, a little flock of wild, green-headed drakes and their speckled brown wives moved in. Linda and Liz, getting off their bus one afternoon, stopped to watch them swimming in the sun. "Aren't they pretty?" said Liz, "especially those blue blue stripes on their wings. How many are there? Two, four, six, seven. That's a lucky number."

A little breeze blew ripples across the pond and dust from the bank into their eyes. Both girls had to brush their eyes clear. "Uh-uh, *six*," Liz corrected herself. "Oh, there's a man watching."

"It's okay. It's only Mr. Chop, the gardener." Linda hoped he would come round the pond and tip his hat to them. She wanted Liz to see how polite he was even to a kid like her.

With some difficulty, Mr. Chop wheeled his bicycle between the bushes. "Afternoon," he said in his soft voice and removed his hat. Liz put out a hand to steady the rake handle, caught among twigs.

Immediately, the ducks paddled furiously across

the water. Quacking and rattling their bills, they converged on the edge and waddled up the bank.

"Run," yelled Liz, running. "They're attacking!"

"N-nonsense," said Linda. "They're only ducks." But she raised her arms to shield her face from flapping wings.

She heard Mr. Chop make soothing clucks in his reedy voice. When she looked again, the little flock was floating peacefully across the pond.

Liz came back. "How did you do that?" she said to Mr. Chop.

He smiled at Liz, hat still in his hand. "I convince them we are among friends. I am sorry if they frighten you." Linda wondered if Liz felt as warmed by his smile as she did, but she was embarrassed to ask the older girl.

When Thanksgiving came, Mr. Chop stopped working. He said the earth must rest for the winter. Linda missed his tip of the hat.

She was glad, though, that old Mrs. Galloway up the street took to feeding cracked corn to the ducks. All winter there were seven of them by the pond. The children waiting for the school bus sometimes threw bits of their sandwiches to them, and Duchess whined at the flock but never chased them.

With spring, the pond ice melted, and the ducks floated again. One afternoon, Linda paused by the

24

water. The ducks splattered and preened, heads under wings. Several turned tail-up. Automatically, Linda counted tail feathers. There were the lucky seven.

A gust of air riffled the water. There was something funny about the wind at the pond. When it blew there, dust flew, but never a tree branch stirred along the road.

"Such a nice sunshine," said a voice behind her. Even though she was glad to see Mr. Chop, Linda jumped, then found herself counting the ducks floating in front of her. Only six. Like Mr. Chop, number seven seemed to come and go. Linda shivered. What she was thinking was *impossible*.

Pulling herself together, Linda made an effort at ordinary conversation. "They look like they're having a good time," she said. Oh, but Mr. Chop did not look so good. He seemed to have grown thin. His vest hung loose. His black-brown eyes looked kind as usual, but grandfatherly now, not princely as she'd thought all fall. His somewhat beaky nose jutted between gaunt cheeks. His green hat needed a good brushing. She'd like to do that for him.

"Is nice you are here," said Mr. Chop. His delighted smile gave Linda that lovely princessy feeling, and she smiled wholeheartedly in return.

Forgetting to be shy, she said, "I missed you this winter."

"So charming you mention," said Mr. Chop. He

25

tipped his hat and bowed toward her.

Each hand holding wide the hem of her skirt, Linda inclined her head to him as if to royalty and dipped an old-fashioned curtsey, deep to the ground.

For a second she stood stunned. Where had she learned *that*? And who did she think she was? Princess Di? Linda turned and ran home where things were dull but normal.

Later that spring, Mr. Chop sent his son Maurice to tend the Hillyers' grass, and clip hedges. At first Mr. Hillyer said, "No more gardeners," but Mrs. Hillyer said she liked the looks of young Maurice.

"Let him stay, Edward. He's not that expensive. You know how pushing a mower bothers your sciatica."

Maurice was up-to-date. He came in a small green truck with his own power mower and, while he also dressed in tan corduroy, buff vest, and white neckerchief; his hat was new plush green.

"Hm, expensive velour," said Mrs. Hillyer of the hat. Maurice, too, doffed it and tipped it with old-fashioned courtesy. Linda smiled at him, the way she had at Mr. Chop, but Maurice was younger and *winked* at her. *Well.*

Linda took to wandering as far as the pond on springish evenings after dinner. One twilight, she stopped to see a batch of baby ducks. They vanished among the tufts at her approach.

"It's a splendid evening, isn't it?" said Mr. Chop at her shoulder.

When Linda faced him, she knew he was thinner than ever, stooped and fragile. She felt sad. "Are you all right?" she said.

"Yes, only my time is almost up. Maurice is acceptable? He has trained a long time. You like him?"

"Sure," said Linda, but she was not at all sure of this conversation. His "time" was "up"? What was Mr. Chop talking about?

"Uh, how long does it take to, to, uh, train a gardener?" she asked. "I mean, like you and Maurice?"

Mr. Chop took out his blue bandanna and wiped his forehead. "It takes a new dimension," he said.

"What?"

"The seen and the unseen. Natures visible and invisible. The worlds beyond."

The air around the pond crackled and felt strange. Prickles ran along Linda's skin. The unseen? The invisible? What other worlds? If you could believe him. Which she could not.

Mr. Chop put the bandanna in his pocket. It was the same blue as the stripes on the mallard's wings. "I must go now." Mr. Chop straightened his shoulders and flexed his elbows. The blue bandanna quivered separately.

Suddenly Linda was afraid to know anything more

about Mr. Chop. "G-good-by," she said and ran till her breath came raw in her throat. She climbed the steps of her porch and sat on the top one. How could she run away from Mr. Chop when she really liked him? Perplexed, she sat so still a sparrow hopped over the flagstones in front of her.

After a time, she noticed Maurice had finished mowing later than usual. Now he was rolling the mower up the ramp into his truck. His vest showed fresh buff chestnut, and even in the fading light his blue bandanna fluttered royal blue.

Relieved at how strong he looked, Linda waved to Maurice. He waved back, then picked up his hat from the seat of the truck and climbed in. He was finished for the day and leaving. As Linda watched, Maurice revved the motor noisily, then drew away from the curb with a squeak of speedy tires.

Oh! Wait! In spite of the dusk, Linda was sure she saw *space* between the tires and the road. As she leaped to her feet, Maurice drove around the turn and out of sight. "Quonk-quonk," drifted back to her; he must have honked his horn to say good-by.

Linda ran to the edge of the lawn and peered around the corner. There was nothing. Maurice had driven away at top speed.

Again, "quonk-quonk," she heard, this time over-head. She looked up at the evening sky. Whatever was up there was an indistinct blur, already disap-pearing in the dusk. Once more, "quonk-quonk," came faintly to her ears, perhaps from the next street. A horn? A bird?

Linda walked back to her front steps and sat down. She folded her hands in her lap and breathed carefully and steadily, in and out. She sat there till her mother called that it was bedtime.

EARLY WINTER:
The Choirmaster

"GOODNIGHT," CARA CALLED.

"See you in the morning, " Liz said as she turned into her front walk.

Cara had to walk further up the Academy Street hill, past the Gilderslieves' enormous house and the Galloways' cottage. The Gilderslieves' dog, Duchess, chased the Galloways' cat, Bluebell, across the street. Cara paused under a streetlight to see how close old Duchess could get. Ten feet. Then the scrambling cat, eyes golden and white fur standing on end, glared from a branch overhead. The dog braced its paws on the trunk and went "Woof."

Cara snapped her fingers. Duchess lolloped over to snuff her glove. "What's new, old Duchess-doggyoh?" sang Cara, because she and Liz had been at the girls' choir practice in St. Luke's. Everyone, including Cara, sang with all-out ardor for the new organist and choirmaster. His name was Paul Shonbrun, and he was the most electric male Cara had ever, in her thirteen years, been aware of. She felt that she alone appreciated Paul Shonbrun's remarkable musical qualities.

He seemed to single her out, too. He had said that evening: "We ought to have a solo voice sometimes. Cara, you first? Try that line, 'Crossing through the tares to thee.' The rest of you hum behind her like the organ. Step forward, Cara."

Mr. Shonbrun's strong white fingers struck chords on the practice piano. He nodded. Cara took a breath and began.

Mr. Shonbrun stopped her almost immediately. "No, no, you're strangling the sound." Of course she was. Her heart leaped into her throat every time he spoke to her.

Mr. Shonbrun placed a hand on her middle. It heated right through her sweater and shirt. "When you get older, you will need lessons to train that voice. Right now, I can tell you, here" — his hand pressed at her rib cage — "you must have control of the diaphragm, to use that open vowel sound that's coming on 'tares.' " Behind, someone giggled.

Letting his hand fall, Mr. Shonbrun grinned at Cara. Cara saw how his hair — worn longer than

Cara's father had his — lay in crisp strands against his shirt collar. "Anybody know what 'tares' are?"

"Sure," said Liz, "junk plants, you know, weeds."

Cara knew she would thrash her way through jungles of weeds to do whatever Paul Shonbrun asked her.

At Sunday's Harvest Home service, to celebrate the coming Thanksgiving, Cara marched with Liz and the others into the church. The boys' choir preceded them, little kids, except for the high school boy who carried the six-foot gilded crucifer. Mr. Shonbrun — you could glimpse him behind the choir stalls, playing the organ. JOY, the treble of the organ seemed to shout, and GLADNESS throbbed the bass keys. JOY, JOY, LIGHT, SHINing LIGHT.

The girls' choir marched two by two. The sun winked through blue and red windows to rainbow their collars.

"Aaa-men," sang the full choir.

"Let us pray," intoned the minister.

Let Paul Shonbrun talk to me at coffee hour, dreamed Cara.

"Remember, there's no practice next week, okay?" was what Paul Shonbrun said to Cara later in the parish house where everyone stood around for after-church coffee. That is, adults drank coffee while the choirs drank Hi-C.

"Of course," said Cara. "It's Thanksgiving. Do you go home for it?" She couldn't stop her eyelashes

32

sort of fluttering at him — he made her so nervous. "Going to have to miss it. Hunting season is open. Bring you back a venison steak?"

"What, oh, deer hunting?" He *killed* animals?

"It's my only chance. The season ends the first of December. For bow and arrow, that is."

He could see she didn't believe him. He dropped his paper cup in a trash basket and pretended to lift a bow and draw the bowstring slowly back to his right ear. "If you have a lot of luck and know what you're doing, *zang*" — he launched an arrow — "you get one of the six points."

"How can you really kill a beautiful deer like that!"

"I only hunt the ones with horns, you know, the big bucks. No mothers or children. Don't worry."

Cara stared into her juice cup.

One of the men asked, "What kind of a bow do you have?"

"Steel bow, tubular, steel-tipped arrows. I use a fiberglass bow for target shooting."

"Ma-an," said Ronald Parris, the state champion choir boy soprano, "I'd like to see that old bow."

"Yes? Keep showing up at choir practice, and maybe I'll bring in the fiberglass some time." The boys' choir met on Wednesday nights.

That was how the long fiberglass bow came to stand in a corner of the parish house the next time they practiced. The bow was as tall as Cara. She smoothed a finger down from the tip.

Mr. Shonbrun hefted it, then fitted the string, which had been loosened, into its slot at one end. He strummed the taut nylon with his thumb. "Feel the balance."

Cara made a face. "I don't like hunting."

"Let me try it," said Liz. Liz never held off on anything.

Mr. Shonbrun gave Liz the bow. He said, "It's more of a challenge than hunting with a gun. If the bow-hunter isn't careful, the bow bites back. Look." He pushed up the sleeve of his shirt — he always took his jacket off first thing — and showed the inside of his wrist. Up to his inner elbow was the yellowing strip of an old bruise.

"That bruise is where the string hit me," he said. "It's got power." Cara could not look at the bruise.

"I'll be careful," said Liz. "Is this right?" She held the bow in her left hand and bent her right elbow as if the bow had an arrow notched.

"That's it, till your hand touches your ear." Mr. Shonbrun nudged Liz's hand farther. Cara frowned. She did not want to handle the bow. She did not want Liz to touch it either, and she especially did not want Mr. Shonbrun to touch Liz that easy way he did.

Liz smirked up at Paul Shonbrun. She was a show-off sometimes. "Do I sight along the arrow to the, well, whatever I'm shooting at?" Liz asked.

Mr. Shonbrun shook his head. "No, the arrow

curves, goes up and then down in its flight. The hunter has to adjust his point of aim to account for it. For instance, let's have a deer, someone. Cara?"

Cara moved slowly in front of them. Mr. Shonbrun took the bow from Liz. "Suppose Cara is off in the brush, but I see her. I don't aim at her shoulders where I want to get 'er, but lower. See the arrow goes up and comes down — *sokko*." Cara twitched and sidled behind the half-open door.

When she hid, Mr. Shonbrun actually chuckled.

After choir was over, Liz and Cara waited together silently for their bus home. They traveled to the Academy Street stop without saying a word. Not till they were going up their hill did Liz say in a voice of wonderment, "To think of Mr. Shonbrun shooting a deer — isn't that just weird?"

"Gross!" said Cara. "It's too gross, you mean."

Liz tossed her hair out of her eyes. "He's still the nicest organist we've ever had at St. Luke's."

Cara left Liz in front of her drive and went on up the hill. She felt an empty space between her ribs. It was as if that had been where she had crammed the fullness of her admiration for Paul Shonbrun. It was not there tonight. She guessed it was because he was stronger and crueller than she had understood. Those perfect white teeth would bite into a deer steak! Cara shuddered.

In the weeks before Christmas, Cara halfheartedly sang Advent hymns with the rest of the girls' choir.

Mr. Shonbrun wanted solos again. He directed Cara to sing. She sang three lines before Mr. Shonbrun crashed his hands on the keys. "Wake up, Cara! Where's that full soprano? When you're older, you'll find singing is worth working at."

Singing ought to be for joy, Cara thought. Mr. Shonbrun made her throw back her shoulders and breathe in and out as if she were a runner.

"Got to let the rafters ring," he said. "You have plenty of power for a kid your age." Cara was not sure she wanted power.

He played the opening chords again and nodded at the rest to begin. Then, at the solo, he lifted his hands high and turned to Cara. "Fly," he commanded.

> *"All the angel-throng*
> *"Hail creation's morning*
> *"With one burst of song."*

Cara's tones soared. She did not recognize herself. That wasn't *her* voice!

Mr. Shonbrun crowed with triumph. "That's *it*. Go for it, girl," he said. Cara did not smile. She felt she had been indecently exposed, even changed into somebody else.

That December, Cara's father said, was the coldest they'd had in a long time. Even Teena, Cara's Siamese, refused to go out. The snow fell early, lots of it. The temperature hovered at twenty degrees and kept the snow white and crisp and even, long into January. The wild deer of the countryside, hungry for greens, invaded peoples' lawns and nibbled at snow-covered rosebushes. Cara found hoofprints like embroidery around their ornamental shrubs. Each print was made of two narrow triangles. They cut into the drifts.

"Isn't that interesting!" said Liz when she came to do homework with Cara. "Deer feet are double, not like a horse, you know. Horses have flat hooves. I think in the old days, when people were superstitious, they thought the devil had separated hooves, cloven they called them, like deer."

Cara shrugged. She had this ugly competitive feeling with Liz these days, and she could not get used to it. She said, "There isn't such a thing as a devil," with real scorn.

Liz giggled.

The *Thorne Center Tribune* ran a story about the deer. It printed a photograph of Mr. Gilderslieve draping hardware cloth over their yew bushes so the deer would not chew on them.

They talked about it at choir practice. Liz said that Mr. Shonbrun should shoot the deer. "Legally," he said, "the season is over." It seemed to Cara that his eyes gleamed wickedly in the light on the piano.

"I thought you ought to know Cara has deer tracks on her lawn," said Liz. Sometimes it occurred to

Cara what Liz thought was remarkable was not at all.

Mr. Shonbrun raised his eyebrows at Cara. "Shall I hide in a bush and take aim?" he said.

"You wouldn't!" breathed Cara and then felt her cheeks rush into hot pink. He was *teasing*. Liz and the others laughed. Pricked with annoyance, Cara noticed for the first time how big Paul Shonbrun's ears were, even a little pointed on top. Like an animal, she thought.

She was forced to think of animals later that evening. Hurrying home, after leaving Liz, she could hear the dog, Duchess, barking. She must have treed Mrs. Galloway's cat again. Cara saw the dog under an oak, surrounded by cat and dog prints in the snow.

Crossly, Cara yelled, "Here, Duchess. Leave Bluebell alone." Cara gazed upward. She put her mitten to her mouth.

There was no Bluebell to be seen anywhere, only a long shaft with feathers that were outlined in the street lamp. Pinned into the tree by the arrowhead was a tuft of white fur.

"Go home, Duchess," said Cara. What other arrows might be flying around the neighborhood? Danger lurked silently behind every tree trunk. Cara shivered and ran home.

She banged the kitchen door behind her. She was grateful to see the ordinary way her mother was drinking tea from a very ordinary mug. Teena sat in her mother's lap.

"I'm quitting choir," Cara said.

"Why is that?"

"Because I want to."

Cara scooped up Teena and carried her to her room. She shut the door and stared into the dark of her window. Her own reflection was there, and the cat's, among the shadowy hemlocks outside in the snow. Needles seemed to decorate her hair as if she, too, lived in the wilderness.

Cara pulled the window shade to the sill. She did not like the wild.

"*Choir is no fun now,*" she said to her cat, and flicked on her bedside lamp. The room was suffused with warm, golden light . . . and safe.

Liz and the others could go right on sucking up to Paul Shonbrun and smirking over his good looks . . . his bows and his arrows, his power and his glorious music.

And his pointed ears.

DEEP WINTER:
Sharooah

As THE NURSE PUSHED ASIDE HIS BREAKFAST TRAY, Streak swung himself around to sit on the edge of the bed. He grabbed his silly hospital shirt to cover himself. "When am I going to run again?" he asked.

"Just dangle your legs, young man," said the nurse.

"I got to get in shape for spring track."

"Mmm. You can talk to doctor about that," said the nurse.

His mother took the day off from her office to drive Streak home from the hospital. They were having a long midwinter cold snap. As Streak sniffed the first fresh air in a long time, his mother said, "Breathe through your scarf."

Streak stood up to walk three steps from the wheelchair to the car. His legs felt leaden, not his own. He stumbled forward and sort of fell into the front seat. The smiling hospital orderly said good-by and took the wheelchair away.

Mrs. Baxter got in the car and tucked a red wool blanket around him. "Imagine having viral pneumonia," she said. "Your brothers never had anything to stump the medical profession. Are you warm enough?"

"Boiling," said Streak and coughed. The heaviness that took over his legs also settled on his chest.

"Shoot me full of penicillin, Doc," Streak had said when he first got sick, "so I get well fast, huh?"

"Sorry," said Dr. Hermann, "no penicillin for viral pneumonia, just lots of rest and good food. Take it slow and easy for a while."

Mrs. Baxter had smiled fondly. "There's never been anything slow or easy about Jason. He's our gold medal runner."

Streak's real name was Jason Carter Baxter. "Streak" was the nickname given him by his older brothers. They said when he was only eight that he ran "like a greased streak."

Streak became his name. He had a runner's build, extra long legs, lean muscles, a slight, tough body, and at thirteen, he was already a county athlete.

But now Streak had to agree to stay quiet at home and do the lessons sent specially for him from Thorne Center junior high.

About to turn into Academy Street, his mother had to slow down to pass a bicyclist pedaling over the snowy road. "It's Jess Kujak!" said Streak. He rolled down his window and yelled, "Hiyah, Jess!" Then he had to cough.

"Put that window up before you catch something else," commanded Mrs. Baxter.

"Can Jess visit after school?"

"I should say not," said his mother. "No tiring visits like that. I'm so relieved your Aunt Berta can stay with you during the day."

"Awww," said Streak. He foresaw days? weeks? of bone-cracking boredom. Great-aunt Berta came for family holidays or emergencies. Streak supposed *he* was considered an emergency. Aunt Berta was old but spry and tough. She'd make certain he'd have no friends, no excitement.

That night he cried himself to sleep. It was being so weak that made him babyish, and he dreamed of losing races.

The next morning Aunt Berta drove up in her sky-blue VW bug. The first thing she did was whip up a milk shake with an egg in it. "I just had breakfast," Streak said. He sat on the couch in the room where he kept his computer.

"You are surely peak-ed-looking," said his great-aunt. "You need more roses in your cheeks. Drink up." Half the shake stuffed him like a sausage.

"After I watch my morning TV, you'll be ready for the rest of it."

"Lay off, Aunt Berta. I'll get sick."

"Ye-es? You're already sick, but I am going to make you as strong as that Mr. America."

"I'd rather run like Carl Lewis," said Streak.

"You'll run soon enough," she said. "Now lie still." She left him on the couch covered with an afghan.

Streak flexed his legs under the cover. He wasn't going to lie cocooned like a caterpillar for long. In a minute he'd get up and put a game on his Apple II.

The morning sun, pouring on the bright snow outside, made extra-thick shadows inside. The baseboard heating around two sides of the room showed a line of deep black shadow along the bottom. In a corner, the darkness flickered.

The darkness flickered?

Streak sat up straight. He stared hard at the corner. Some little speck of shadow slid along, under the baseboard cover. A mouse? Streak smiled at the swiftness of such a tiny animal. He saw something approach the half-open door, then slip under the crack. Must be an awful skinny mouse. Streak waited for Aunt Berta to shriek.

Minutes passed. No yells from the kitchen. Must be she never glimpsed it.

43

Here — something in the crack under the door flowed toward him and Streak said, "Hey!" right out loud. "Hey, mouse!"

A thin, high-pitched whistling rasped at his ears. It said . . . no, it couldn't have, but somehow Streak distinctly heard *words* . . . "Not a mouse."

Without thinking, Streak answered, "If you're not a mouse, what are you — a mole?" and could not believe it when the same whistly voice replied, "Pah! Those overweight, awkward beasts!"

Streak pinched his wrist. He *was* awake. He cleared his throat. His voice did not want to work right. "I thought moles were pretty small," he managed.

"Big-nosed ponderosities," squeaked the shadow. "*I* am streamlined and beautiful, swifter than light." It whisked around the hearth tiles and hid in the darkness beneath the radiator.

"Then what *are* you? How did you get in? Where are you going? Where do you live? Where did you run to, just now? Why do I understand you?"

Angry high chittering. "Pestering questions. Questioning pesterer. Time-wasting *boy*."

Streak kicked his legs free of the afghan and knelt by the radiator baseboard. He laid his head sidewise on the rug to peer underneath. Why wouldn't it answer questions?

Whistling came from the far corner where the heating pipe went through the floor to the basement furnace. "Slo-ow. Toobig. Big much too slow. Can't

44

catch me." The raspy whistling words faded, and Streak remained on the floor, trying to see — something.

"What are you doing on the floor, Jason? You don't feel faint, do you?" Aunt Berta put down the half-glass of milk shake and hurried to help Streak up from his hands and knees.

Streak waved her off and got up. "I'm fine, just inspecting the, ah, the heating system." Then he had to sit down because he'd stood up too fast and gotten a little dizzy. It shocked him to be so out of condition.

Aunt Berta put the glass in his hand. Streak gave a pull on the straw. "What's small as a mouse, faster than a mole?" he asked.

"We have a mouse? I'll buy a trap," said Aunt Berta.

"No, no, no mice, no trap!" said Streak.

"Well, " said the old lady, and she took away the empty glass.

Streak put his Kung Fu Masters disc in the computer to play a game. Ugh! His reaction time was slower than it had ever been. Usually he could beat his friends, but he felt the hospital had slowed him down. Or maybe, like that funny little mouse-thing said, he was too big to be fast.

Morosely, he put away the disc and shut off the machine. He was really sick of being sick.

He got down beside the radiator again and sighted

along it. Where the pipe went down was a semicircular gap big enough to slip through — that is, if you were small, like this animal. Streak imagined that climbing down a heating pipe for a mouse-sized creature would be like a person cliff-climbing in the Sierras. Wow!

"I think you and that floor have something in common," said his aunt, "like you're both *down* as they say."

Streak rolled over on his back and giggled. He looked up at Aunt Berta who carried a green-laquered tray. "Lunch already?"

"Go wash your hands now you've been on that floor," she said. "We don't need any more germs."

When he returned, his aunt sat and observed his first few mouthfuls of hamburger. Streak said, "It's very good, Aunt Berta. Thank you."

"You're so welcome, Jason. Just eat and get well." She got up and ran a hand over his hair, then left.

"Meat!"

Streak stopped chewing to make sure he heard what he thought he'd heard. He looked toward the corner radiator pipe. He thought that shrill whistle said "meat."

The same slight, velvety shadow flowed toward him. "Impolite not to share."

Streak broke off a crumb and knelt to place it in front of the shadow.

The creature slipped away and down the gap be-

side the pipe, leaving the hamburger grain un-
touched. "Not so close, boy. I bite." The whistle
squealed with a hollow sound from between the
floorboards.

"Sorry," said Streak and wanted to giggle. This
cross little being that wouldn't answer questions or
let him get close struck him as funny as Saturday
cartoons. The great thing about it was that it was
real.

In a few minutes, the creature, all two inches of
it, approached the hamburger, ate rapidly, then
cleaned its mouth with tiny paws. "Quite heart-
ening."

Streak tossed a crust of roll with butter on it. The
animal pounced, devouring butter up to its whiskers.

"Please," Streak said, "just what are you?"

Unfortunately, the animal's mouth was glued with
butter as it answered, "Hroo, a course."

Streak could not understand the answer. "What?"
he said.

"Stoomanyqueshuns," it snarled nastily. Streak de-
cided names were not as important as keeping this
creature for company. He offered instead some in-
formation about himself. "My name's Streak," he
said. There was no reaction. He tried again. "Have
some more meat?"

This time, a beady little eye, maybe the size of a
glittery poppy seed, fastened on him, and the whistle
said, "Prefer rare, you know."

"Sure," Streak said, "me too."

"The bloodier the better." Streak broke off a pink section but stifled a bubble of laughter in his throat. He did not want to offend this, this prickly personality. Having it around sure made the time he had to spend getting well pass a lot quicker.

The animal, such a deep dark gray velvet it seemed almost black, demolished the red meat. "Too cold weather outside," it whistled. "Why I came. Earth frozen too deep. Can't pry out beetle grubs. Hope ice melts next month so can dig food properly. Scavenging crumbs . . . undignified."

Streak considered the creature as it recleaned its whiskers. He really liked the definite way it spoke, and the way it seemed to challenge everything, even the weather. Streak enjoyed challenges himself. That was one of the fine parts about running races.

While he was thinking, the little thing disappeared. Streak ate his carrot sticks but saved an end. He also saved a marblesized lump of the rarest beef and a crumb of roll. He heaped the food in the middle of the rug on a corner of his paper napkin. Because Streak needed company, he was determined to keep this cranky midget returning for more. Who knows? It might even get to like him a little.

Shortly, the creature emerged from its gap and pointed its slender nose toward Streak's offering. "Picnic?" said the high raspy voice and fell upon the hamburger grains. Streak grinned with the pleasure of being generous. But, "Whatzis?" it said, mouth full, paw on carrot.

"The end of my carrot stick."

The creature picked it up. It turned the fragment over and over. It was big as a beach ball might be to Streak. "Insufficient protein," came the whistle. It dropped the carrot.

"I'm not crazy about vegetables, either," said Streak.

"Eat to live is what I do. Eat fast. Live fast."

Streak smiled wryly. "I used to be darn fast myself," he said. "I'm a runner. I won ribbons, got a silver cup. Right now, I've had to slow down. It's awful."

"Yes. Terrible cold weather," said the animal. "Drafty in tunnels. Hardly moving fast myself."

Streak asked, "Is it fun running through tunnels? Like on Hallowe'en night when you can't tell what's just around the corner?"

"Not acquainted hollow ween. Try tunneling and see." The creature humped along to the corner pipe. It never sat still.

"Wait, wait. How could I possibly try it, try tunneling the way you say?"

"Think small," came the irritated whistle. "Small is beautiful," it squeaked and disappeared.

Streak sat back chagrined. Alone again. He reinserted Kung Fu Masters. Now if he were the size of one of those figures on the monitor, he'd be about right to climb down a heating pipe. He fell asleep, smiling, head on the computer keyboard.

On Saturday evening, Mr. and Mrs. Baxter were going out. "Maybe I should call a baby-sitter," fretted his mother, "because Aunt Berta is busy this evening."

After Streak and his father convinced his mom that Streak was well enough to be left alone, Streak promised to be in bed by ten. He looked forward to an empty house. It occurred to him that his come-and-go visitor might be more at ease without bigger people around.

After supper Streak sat in front of his computer with a game on. He waited. He intended to find out exactly what this tiny animal was, and for sure what it meant by "think small." He piled a batch of Aunt Berta's finest cookies on top of his computer table. He knew he'd need a bribe.

With the machine humming, Streak hardly noticed the creature's return. It surprised him. It flowed up the leg of his chair and broad-jumped from the armrest to the computer table. "Hey!" said Streak. A little frightened, he shoved himself against the back of his chair. After all, it did say it could bite.

The creature mounted the keyboard and glared at the screen, its tiny paws balled into fists. "Interlopers!" it snarled and struck at the figures on the monitor.

Streak had to smile. "They aren't real. They're only

on a computer disc. They're my Kung Fu Masters. It's only a game of martial arts."

"Marshall Artz? Then I'm General Shrew!" The beast slid down the chair leg to the floor and started to run. Probably for the kitchen crumbs, Streak thought.

He waved an oatmeal cookie through the air. "Better crumbs in here," he said. "Is that your name? General Shrew?"

"Obtuse adolescent!" said the animal, but stopped and turned back at the hearth. "Making joke. Ha ha. I am called Common Shrew, see? Crumb?"

Streak tossed a large chunk of cookie. "I never figured out what you are."

"Already said!"

"But your mouth was full, and I couldn't understand you. I never saw a shrew before." Streak broke off a piece of walnut and rolled it toward the shrew.

Tiny smackings and slurpings preceded an impatient order: "Look under S encyclopedia," it whistled. The tone of voice reminded Streak of his school librarian.

Streak went to the living room and brought in the *P–Sim* volume from the bookcase. He turned the pages. " 'Insectivorous mammal,' " he read aloud.

"Hah. Insects in deep freeze," came the squeal. "Desperate winter."

" 'A nervous, active animal, it is a prodigious eater and vicious fighter.' "

51

"That is I, voracious, quick on the trigger. Treat me with respect." Streak saw that the shrew sat up and stroked its narrow plush chest with tiny paws.

He read further: " 'The heart of the common shrew beats eight hundred times a minute.' "

The shrew was so excited it jumped up and down. "Faster than hummingbird, faster than sound, that is I, her Superswiftness, Sharooah."

Sharooah? Her? Now he not only knew what she was but that she had her own name. "Sharooah," he coaxed, "how can I 'think small,' the way you said, so I can run with you?"

"Con-cen-trate. Condense. *In*-ten-si-fy to essence. More tasties?"

Streak felt around the edge of his cookie and broke off a raisin. He tossed it.

Chomp chomp. "Big animal needs to sink into center Self like a raisin."

"Wha-at?" Streak laughed. "A raisin? You mean dry up? Well, thanks a lot!"

"No." The shrew looked steadily at Streak. "Sharooah most appreciative of feast. Telling you how to sink into Self. Must implode."

Streak wished the shrew did not use such big words. "I never heard of implode."

"*Stupido!* Mean fold into smallest Self. Like a raisin."

Streak rubbed his nose. "Well, light and dry and airy, I guess you mean." He thought harder. "Funny, when I've run my best, I know I concentrate real hard like that."

"Think running then."

"Yeah? Running's great. My legs never ache or my breathing hurts till the race is over, you know? Sharooah?" No reply. Tears, always near the surface since the hospital, made Streak's nose water. He rubbed it fiercely on his sleeve.

It was so important to him: He knew that if he could dash through new places, if he did not have to feel his body or the chair under his legs nor the sweater over his shoulders, then he could feel himself again, the way he used to, strong and in control.

Streak took a deep breath. Don't be a baby, he urged himself. He unwrapped his special treat from a napkin, one of Aunt Berta's rich chocolate brownies, crammed with almonds and frosted with iced coconut. He placed it in the middle of the floor.

In a while he heard crunches of coconut. "Simply scrumptious," said the familiar whistle, and for the first time, "Thank you."

Pleased, Streak said, because he'd heard Aunt Berta say it, "A dish fit for a king, huh?"

"For Princess Sharooah, yes." Munch munch.

"You're a *princess*?"

" 'Course. Princess Royal."

"Really?" Streak did not believe it but kept himself very polite just in case.

"Maybe Sharooah needs to share royal tunnels.

Noblesse oblige, you know. Ready to reward too-big creature for multitudes of banquets. Sharooah will help you to grow small tonight. Run into terminal condensation."

Streak's eyes widened. Not sure of what "terminal condensation" might be, except that it sounded computer-friendly, he sensed a readiness in himself to burst into speed. "You mean I get to run with you?"

"Yes, after running jump into smallness," said Sharooah. "Nimble-quick."

Streak's heart settled into the steady driving thump he was used to before a track meet. The excitement of anticipation drove him to say, "All *right*. That'll be so neat." His voice broke on "neat," and his throat went dry. He had not exactly made up his mind yet, had he? But with Sharooah, one couldn't delay. She could switch *her* mind, royal or otherwise, in a flash, and then he'd never run in a royal tunnel.

So when she commanded, "Close eyes," he did. "Now, run out of your gross world."

Streak tried to squeeze himself weightless as a wrung-out sponge and imagined himself running at the start of a relay. His feet hit air, and he was falling, plummeting downward. It felt like dropping in an elevator from the top of a skyscraper. As he fell, he could also see himself as if he were two bodies . . . one observing the other, going down, smaller and smaller.

"Plunge out of Personhood," whistled Sharooah. When Mr. and Mrs. Baxter returned home quite late, they discovered Streak was not in his bed. His mother found him on the couch near his computer, sound asleep, she thought. "Don't wake him, John," she said to Mr. Baxter. "He needs his rest. I'll cover him and let him sleep in here."

But Sunday morning, when she went to wake Streak, she saw he was sprawled as if he'd never moved all night. He seemed empty as a husk, one arm hanging lifeless and the fingers awkwardly brushing the rug. When she could not rouse him, she had hysterics.

Mr. Baxter telephoned the police and fire emergency, but Aunt Berta arrived first, after early church. She put Mrs. Baxter back to bed and then went to Streak. She picked him up and cradled his cast-off shape on her lap. "MMmmmhmmmhm," Aunt Berta hummed, as if he were a baby.

Two tiny animals flowed out of the crescent around the radiator pipe and looked up at her. The old lady did not notice. The larger one whistled, "I'll go back now."

"Never back," squeaked the other. "Always forward."

While the shrews watched, a tear ran down the old lady's cheek. "No!" said the bigger one. "I did not know how sad she'd be. Now I got to Think Big." He snapped his teeth at the smaller animal.

55

"No need to bite," said Sharooah. "Go."

Streak did not have to "think running" to return to the bigger world. Imploding, exploding, or whatever he'd done before never entered his mind. Loving Aunt Berta was enough to get him exactly where he wanted to go.

He felt as if every little muscle, every nerve end and artery twitched to a new beat. A zillion tiny sunbeams coursed through his body and swelled bigger . . . bigger . . . *boy*. Streak struggled to sit upright on Aunt Berta's bony lap.

The old lady let out a screech of happiness and tried to hug the very breath out of him. His parents came running. Disheveled, dressed in their faded old bathrobes, they sure looked beautiful to him.

Streak felt fine for the first time in weeks. "What's going on?" he asked.

His parents, open-mouthed, and Aunt Berta seemed paralyzed with surprise.

As if to break a spell, Streak hollered, "I'm hungry, *starving*. What's for breakfast?"

Then suddenly, all of them were crying and laughing at the same time. Streak reached up to wipe Aunt Berta's cheek. Oops, how did his hands get so grubby? Did he think it or say it?

"Running on all four paws of course," came a whistle. "Farewell, boy."

MARCH:
The Shirt

LUCY KNEW THAT GRAMPS HAD MORE GREAT IDEAS about things to do than anyone else could think of in a month of Sundays. That was one of his funny old sayings, "a month of Sundays." Nothing ever lagged or went colorless and dull with boredom when Gramps got an idea. Look at that summer he'd had the sailboat on the river. He'd given Lucy a cap that spelled out CREW across the visor. They had super sails together.

Even before the Marilyn G., there had been the chemistry set her mother would not allow her to play with. Gramps gave it to her when she was eight. She had to play with it in Grandmother Galloway's kitchen on Academy Street because Lucy's mother objected. "I don't have time to clean up after you. Chemicals can stain those white tiles when you spill." Lucy's mom worked as Dr. Tobias's dental assistant every afternoon but Tuesdays.

"Bring it to our house, Luce," Gramps had said. Grandfather Galloway lived on Academy Street. So with her friend Lisa, in the Galloway kitchen they had made rotten egg smells, and coated pennies with silver. Once they thought they'd made gunpowder by mistake and blown up the experiment with a great *boom.* It was only Gramps who had exploded a blown-up paper bag to tease them. They all had a good laugh.

So when Lucy came into the final week of her sixth grade sewing class, her mother still wasn't around much to help. Right away Lucy knew she'd go to Academy Street for help, because she loved her grandmother's sewing machine. It was one of Gramps's marvels. Gramps had found it at a flea market, an old pedal Singer, and he had lugged it home and wired it to a motor, cleaned it, regilded it, and made it user-friendly. It did not crouch, stern and efficient, the way the school sewing machines did. Those waited to spring at Lucy with some terrible rip-that-out mistake. With interminable double French seams, Lucy had ripped out so many, so often, the man's shirt she was supposed to produce was peppered all over with needle markings. Up and down the sleeves, back and forth across a part called

58

a yoke, the thick material showed empty holes where stitches had come out. Every time Lucy went to sewing class, she felt her eyes fill with unshed tears of frustration. There would never be an end to that gruesome shirt!

"I need to take my sewing to Academy Street," said Lucy.

"Well-l-l," said her mother, "you know they've moved your grandfather into that room where your grandmother has the sewing machine. Because it's on the ground floor."

"I know, but he'll get better now that he's home from the hospital."

"Call your grandmother."

When telephoned, Grandmother said, "Good. Do come. I know your company will help cheer up Gramps."

After school, Lucy put the pieces of blue denim into a plastic bag and took the bus to Academy Street. She had to walk more than halfway up the hill to Gramps's house. When she passed the Gilderslieves', all those Gilderslieve kids were milling around on the side lawn.

"Luc-cee!" yelled Adrienne, who was in her class. "C'mon play Statues." Beth Gold was there, too. She was always where Adrienne was, willing to play some stupid game like Statues.

Lucy shook her head. "I'm behind in sewing," she said. "I have to work at my grandparents'."

"That sewing glop," said Adrienne.

Though Lucy hated sewing, she proudly lifted her chin. "It'll be super on their machine. Everything is." Lucy was that confident about anything her grandfather had worked on. Head erect, she walked up the hill.

After Adrienne's there was a long gap of trees, and then, after the Nerones', was her grandparents' little house. Lucy walked around the gravel circle, where Gramps had placed a pole and halyard for displaying flags. He'd often flown the American flag up top and the colors from the Marilyn G. below it. Neither flapped there now.

Lucy rang the bell. Her grandmother opened the door. "Just in time for tea and toast. I'm making a pot for your grandfather. Is this the sewing project?"

Lucy nodded. "Can I see Gramps?"

"Go right in," and then in a lower tone, "He gets gloomy being so long in bed. Don't be afraid if he seems changed to you."

It was impossible to be *afraid* of Gramps. Lucy wrinkled her short nose and tossed her blonde hair over one shoulder. What was Grandmother talking about?

Lucy walked through the dining room with its tall stiff chairs, though the swinging door to the kitchen and down a back hall to a big sunny room. In the middle wall of the room reared an enormous shiny brass bedstead. Almost as white as the pile of pillows behind him, her grandfather was propped, tiny and wizened.

Lucy stumbled over the threshold. Had he always been that small? His eyes were closed. She whispered, "Are you asleep, Gramps?"

She took a step toward the bed, already tentative about disturbing him. His right hand, lying on the bright quilt, hardly dented the puffed-up patterns. She could see the blue veins through his white skin. If she kissed him very, very carefully . . . ?

Lucy rested her knuckles on the bed and bent to his cheek.

"BOO!" said her grandfather through his brush of mustache. Lucy jumped a foot.

Grandfather's eyes flew open, as blue as blue sky on a summer's day with a bright white sail behind him. "Gotcha," he said. His voice held the satisfied lilt it used to have when he frightened her out of hiccups.

Lucy had to giggle. "Gramps, you're better."

"Yup. Not exactly full speed ahead, but by gadfrey we're tacking crosswind," he said. He had to struggle to sit straighter.

Lucy glanced away. If she did not look at him, if she only heard his slightly gravelly voice, he seemed like the grandfather she'd known all her life.

Grandma entered. "Now then, a nice cup of tea, E. J., and cinnamon toast. There's a boiled egg. Lucy, hold the tray while I get him up higher."

61

Lucy held the tray. Besides what must be toast under a silver warming bell, there was a blue and white egg cup with an egg sitting upright. Egg scissors rested on the plate. Lucy chewed her underlip. Her grandfather loved thick slices of ham and two fried eggs, over easy. That boiled egg was the stuff they gave sick people.

Gramps, himself, resented it. While Grandma got him under the arms and hoisted him against the pillows, Gramps growled, "I don't want that damned pap, Marilyn."

"Ttssh," said Grandma. She put another pillow across Gramps's lap and settled plate and egg cup on it.

"Thank you, Lucy. Put the tray on the bureau, dear. Now, I'll help you with the egg, E. J., so you don't get yolk on your mustache."

"Whoah," Gramps said, "always tucking these foul extras into my insides. Lucy wouldn't eat one of these confounded runny eggs at four o'clock in the afternoon, would you, Luce?" Studiously, Lucy poured tea into three cups. She took one.

"Doctor's orders," said Grandma. Lucy watched her dip up a slippery-looking spoonful of egg which she thrust between Gramps's lips.

"Aarrgh. Don't feed me. Gi' me that spoon." Gramps dribbled a yellow line down his chin. Lucy grimaced on his behalf.

She put down her teacup and walked to the corner

of the room where the old sewing machine sat up-right on its stand. The broad pedal of scalloped iron was positioned an inch or two off the floor and balanced on a bar that ran between convoluted and much-decorated iron legs. There were full-blown roses worked into the middle of the curlicues and leaves. A sphinx painted in gold lay along the upper body of the machine. The wheel that you pushed gently to get the Singer into motion shone like silver from multitudes of gentle pushes.

Lucy understood the old machine was part and parcel, as he'd say himself, of her grandfather. When Gramps had electrified it and hung the motor under the golden oak top, he had patted the wire coils with a loving hand. As one's foot pressed the pedal, the wires from the motor fed electricity to the needle and zipped stitches a mile a minute. Sometimes the motor unit spat sparks and smelled of ozone. That was exciting and scary. Gramps cheered the sparks. "Enough power there to run a steamship," he liked to say.

Now Lucy spread out the pieces of the shirt, basted together in long wobbly stitches. There were the back yoke and the two sleeves. And the cuffs and the collar. It was worse than any jigsaw puzzle she and Gramps had ever tackled. Lucy held up a sleeve. "I have to sew up the sleeve first?"

"Mmm," said Gramps, "doesn't seem right for a splice yet. You can't sew a round tube like a sleeve into a flat shoulder, can you?" Without turning, Lucy knew that Gramps was blowing crumbs through his mustache.

"Okay, so I *don't* sew up the sleeve. Instead, well, I ought to sew the sleeve *flat* into this *flat* yoke thing?"

"Seems reasonable," said Gramps. "Any more of that toast, Marilyn?"

That worked out all right, and Lucy had the old machine humming. Behind her, Gramps hummed, too, then broke into a whistled melody. "Going to feel fit as a fiddle soom," he said. Lucy grinned.

Then, she realized she had forgotten to sew the sleeve right side out to allow for turning it inside out for a French seam, or was it the other way around? Rats!

"This shirt is very complicated," Lucy complained as she ripped away at the completed, but incorrect, seam. "All this turning inside and outside and ripping . . . I'll have to come back tomorrow and work some more, Gramps."

"Hope so, Luce," said her grandfather. Lucy saw that pink colored his cheeks. His nose seemed less beaky over his mustache. "Always did make me feel real chipper to watch another human being labor while I rested."

The next afternoon, she made more headway on the shirt, and Gramps ate two boiled eggs. Lucy sewed the back to the yoke and, clipping the thread away, held the shirt up for Gramps to see.

He clapped his hands. "An A-number-one shirt," he said. "Lots of pizzazz left in that old machine. Who gets to wear that classy item, Lucy?"

"Mrs. Janner says we donate them to the Red Cross. They give them to flood victims and needy people."

"Shucks. I guess I'm not needy enough."

"Two of you could fit into this shirt, Gramps."

"Too true. I seem to be shrinking these days."

She had not meant that. "Oh-oh," she said and peered at the latest seam. "I have to rip tonight where I kind of swung out of line. Mrs. Janner won't pass crooked seams. I'll have to come back tomorrow."

"Good," said Gramps. "Keep the ozone sparking, sweetheart. Makes the air smell sweeter to me."

Next afternoon, Lucy held up the shirt against the light. "Oh dear! You can see every mistake. The denim is so heavy, you can see light through the holes I left ripping out stitches. Who'd want a shirt full of holes like that?"

"That's a star shirt, Lucy. Hoist it again."

For the second time, Lucy held the shirt to the light so the empty holes showed brightly through the fabric.

" 'Sgreat," said Gramps. "That shirt is a constellation of stitches, practically a Milky Way of twinkles."

"But those are *mistakes*," said Lucy. "It's where I

had to keep ripping out the stitches that went wrong. Nobody else in class has so many ripped-out seams, not even Adrienne Gilderslieve. I think Beth helps her."

"I like those star tracks," said Gramps, and he chuckled at his own joke. He was eating poached eggs on buttered toast.

Lucy returned and returned to Gramps's bedroom. She even grew to enjoy her mistakes because Gramps did. As the sewing machine motor spat and sparked, Gramps's eyes sparkled, and the pink grew in his cheeks. In the afternoons, she and Gramps were partners again, as they'd been on the Marilyn G. Lucy observed, "No wonder Mrs. Janner calls this a work shirt. All I do is *work* on it."

"Ha ha!" There came a deep belly laugh from the bed. Lucy had not heard Gramps laugh like that in a long time.

"Go to it, Luce," urged Gramps. Lucy pressed the pedal harder, and the motor whirred, the needle flashing in the light.

The afternoon came when the seams were straight and even. Lucy clicked the motor off. She felt a funny shiver, but she spoke cheerily. "There, I think it's really, really done." She lifted the needle away from the bobbin plate.

"Uh-huh," agreed Gramps. His legs shifted under the sheets. Lucy held up the shirt for Gramps to admire, but his eyes were closed.

"Tell your grandmother to come in when you go, Luce." Oh, so she was leaving? She might as well.

Lucy left the shirt at home one more day. She wanted to iron it before she handed it in. When she returned from school that Tuesday, her mother had left a note propped by the phone about going to her grandparents'; an "emergency," the note said. "Back for supper." Her mother's handwriting was so scrawly she must have written in a big hurry. Why?

Lucy bit her lip and thought. She remembered the last emergency at her grandparents' was when the freezer broke down in August. She had helped carry frozen foods to the Nerones' next door. Whatever it was, Gramps would tell them what to do.

Relieved at the idea, Lucy got the iron and spread the shirt. She ironed very carefully, as if her care could erase any crisis over on Academy Street. Pressing down hard, she saw that nothing was going to obliterate those pricked holes of mistakes. Well, stars, Gramps had called them. Lucy so much wanted him to see the shirt, ironed and beautifully packaged.

She folded the shirt into tissue paper and placed it in an old birthday box. When she got to her grandparents', the door was opened by a neighbor. "Oh, Lucy," said Mrs. Pennell. "Was your mother expecting you?"

Why was Liz's mother answering the doorbell? Lucy stepped under her extended arm and into the hall. She would have gone farther, but Mrs. Pennell put a hand on her wrist. "Wait here, honey. I'll tell your mother."

Her mother hurried in and put her arms around Lucy for a quick hug. "Lucy, dear. I said I'd be back for supper. Didn't you see my note?"

"Sure. I wanted to come, too. I want Gramps to see my shirt. I ironed it." Lucy clutched the shirt box to her chest so hard that a corner dug into her ribs. It must be that that made her feel so breathless.

"I have something sad to tell you." Lucy's mother paused. "It's, well, your grandfather is dead." Her mother cleared her throat. "I know how unhappy you must feel, but he was quite ill. Now we know he's at rest." Her mother's voice, which had wobbled on "rest," stopped.

Lucy still could not breathe right. She backed toward the door.

Her mother asked, "Where are you going, dear?"

"Out," said Lucy in a flat voice. Her lungs seemed too squeezed to say more.

Her mother tried to hug Lucy again, just as the box dropped to the floor. Lucy bent to pick it up. "Then wait for me at home?" Her mother seemed anxious.

"All right." Lucy moved automatically. Her feelings were frozen with disbelief. She closed the door behind her very quietly. She did not go home. She sat on the front steps and looked out over the lawn and the gravel. Way down the hill, the Gilderslieves whooped.

The halyard on Gramps's flagpole clanked its brass hooks in the little breeze. Lucy opened her box and shook out the shirt. She walked to the flagpole. She unwound Gramps's neat hank of rope, anchored to its wooden cleat, and hauled down the hooks. Concentrating, she fitted the hooks through each cuffed sleeve.

With a pull, she had the shirt rising up the pole like a blue pennant that billowed with the moving air. The shirt was Gramps's anyway, and there, you could see the light, like pinpricks of stars, through the denim.

Guiding the rope slowly, she lowered the shirt halfway down the pole. Half-staff for a death, he'd told her.

She'd get an "incomplete" in sewing. She did not care. She wished she had just gone on with crooked seams and ripping and leaving more constellations of stitches, the way he'd said. Her biggest mistake was finishing the shirt.

Tears slid down her cheeks and dripped off her chin. If only Gramps could see his star shirt fly.

APRIL:
Rearview Vision

As THEY TRUDGED OUT FROM TOWN, CHRIS CAR-
ried his lacrosse stick under one elbow and drained
his can of soda. He laid the emptied Dr Pepper into
the lacrosse netting pocket and grinned toward his
brother on the other side of the street. "Yours," he
said and arced the can to Jeff.

The can clattered on the pavement. "No littering,"
said Jeff. He crushed Chris's can with one foot and
tipped his own soda for the last drops.

"See you," Jeff said and tossed his can toward
Chris's pocket. Chris caught it neatly.

"Way to go." Chris cradled the can and trotted
ahead.

Sweaty and rumpled, in lacrosse team red shorts

and T's, they looked more alike than they usually did. They were fraternal twins, not identical, Liz said. She was their younger sister and a stickler for the right words.

The two continued walking along Prince Street and tossing the can over the occasional car. They had had a pickup game at the school recreation field. "Cross over . . . nothin's comin'," said Jeff, who walked backward. As they turned from Prince into Pond Road, they could see three red emergency flares set into the shoulder of the road, and two police cars parked with lights twirling.

"Live action!" said Chris. "Somebody's really had it."

"Look at the Merce," said Jeff. "How'd he do that?"

A large Mercedes, diesel, straddled the chain highway fence. Its rear axle was hoisted so high that a wheel hung free and slowly revolved. On its side, opposite, lay a long white sporty-looking two seater. "Not exactly the usual Thorne Center jalopies," said Jeff.

In the middle of the road, circling one another, were what must have been the two drivers. A policeman stepped between the two men, and another officer clamped onto the collar of the bigger guy's red jacket. "Let's cool it, buddy," he said.

The big guy shouted, "Tailgating and making faces! I saw him in my mirror!"

71

"The idiot pulled right out in front of me!" squawked the other. "No time to brake even. Got what he deserved."

Chris thought the big guy looked ready to bawl. "My brand new Mercedes, just shipped from Germany. That nerd tried to cream it!"

Chris put the butt of his stick on the macadam and leaned his chin on the pocket rim. Jeff dropped the empty can they had been playing with. It rattled with a tinny scrape on the pavement. The first policeman noticed them. "Going home, boys?"

"Yeah," Chris said.

"No need to loiter," said the officer. "Just keep on going home, fellas." He lifted his walkie-talkie to speak to somebody downtown.

"Got the message," said Jeff. "C'mon Chris." As the boys walked past the crippled Mercedes, Jeff leaned down and picked up something from the wayside litter.

"Never mind that junk," said Chris. "I'm in a hurry for a shower." He walked ahead faster so they were single file. His back toward his twin, Chris did not see him blow the dust from a bright shining square of glass set into a gleaming rim.

After giving it a rub, Jeff slid the exterior rearview mirror, which was what it was, under his T-shirt. It felt hot and cold at the same time and made a bulge where his stomach was flat. He kept a hand on it.

When they came to Academy Street and started

uphill, Chris joined his brother, and of course noticed the lump. "What's keeping your belly warm, huh?"

Jeff took the bulge from under his shirt and let it spin between thumb and index finger. It was a large outside mirror all right, cleanly sheared off an outside mounting.

"One of those guys'll need that," said Chris.

"Nah. It's broken the fastener. Had to come off the Merce," said Jeff. "Same paint. Heavy sucker, isn't it?" The mirror was bigger than a handspan. The glass itself seemed extraordinarily clear, and flashed in the afternoon sunlight as Jeff rotated it.

"Wick-*ed*," Chris said and stepped close to gaze into it. Both had been smiling, Chris with his one chipped tooth, and Jeff with the scratch on his chin, but as they stared together into the mirror, it was as if the sun hid under a cloud. The freckles on Chris's nose stood out, and the tooth kind of snaggled in his reflection.

Jeff jutted his jaw into the mirror and grinned so fiercely his teeth showed, clenched. His hand holding the mounting tensed to a fist. "Quit shovin'," he growled. "Who found this anyway?"

Chris reached for the mirror. Jeff jerked it, but they both continued to stare into it. Chris lifted his lip like a snarling dog. "Crud! This belongs to the Mercedes, not you." Chris made another grab at the mirror and got his hand around Jeff's. He lifted his lacrosse stick and gave Jeff a sharp rap on the knuckles.

"Ouch," said Jeff and dropped the mirror in some weeds.

Chris stepped away. He felt dumb. They hardly ever fought, and certainly over nothing as inconsequential as a busted-off mirror. "Sorry, Jeff," he said.

"No problem," said Jeff. He fished the heavy rectangle from the bunch of dandelion stems and wiped the glass on the front of his shirt. Without really looking at it, he put it in his lacrosse pocket. He carried it that way, shaft tight under his elbow to offset the weight. The mirror was too big for the pocket and poked up to wink in the last of the afternoon sun.

"It's okay, finders keepers," said Chris genially. "Race you for the shower." He ran up the hill and into their house.

Jeff followed. He stopped in the room he shared with Chris and stood his stick in the corner. He listened to Chris already yodelling in the shower and dropped the mirror upside down on his bed. Why did he insist on bringing it home? When they were little, they had collected useful junk from most anywhere, but they'd long grown out of that, hadn't they? Jeff shivered. He needed that hot shower. "Hurry up," he yelled at the door of their shared bath. He stripped off his T-shirt and threw it toward the bed. It collapsed over the mirror. On impulse,

Jeff wrapped his new acquisition in the soiled T-shirt and shoved it under the bed. There. Out of sight, out of mind. He'd think about what he wanted to do with it later.

But he did not think about the mirror soon enough. The high school junior who came to clean on Wednesday, hauled it out when her vacuuming caught at the shirt. His mother told him about it after school. "At least Annabel finished that room before she left," his mother said. "I don't know what came over her. She went into some sort of fit about what was under your bed and then just took off. I haven't had a chance to check because I had to clean the rest of the house myself."

Jeff went up to his room. On the floor at the edge of his bed was his T-shirt with the mirror, unwrapped, lying in the middle of it. Suppose the vacuum scratched that perfect crystal? Jeff knelt and ran the tips of his fingers over the glass. It was okay.

Still on his knees, he looked around wondering what had upset Annabel. A dirty T-shirt and a car mirror would not have sent her home in a tizzy the way his mother said. Unless she were an awfully neat girl or something.

His mother entered the room and saw the dirty shirt first thing. "Jeff, you know filthy clothing belongs in the laundry. And what do you want with that big car mirror, broken off like that?" She stood and looked down into the glass.

Jeff also glanced into the mirror and caught his mother's reflection as she glanced at his jersey. He was shocked at how witchlike his own mother seemed. Usually the twins thought their mother looked pretty nice. Jeff did not like it at all that now she *glared* at him in the mirror, face drawn and angry. Her eyes were hard enough to strike sparks.

To hide that threatening expression, Jeff flipped the mirror facedown. "Don't be so mad, Mom. I'm sorry I forgot the shirt." When he stood up and faced her, she only smiled and looked loving again. She left after rumpling his hair.

This mirror — it somehow bothered Annabel? It seemed to bother Mom though she only complained of the shirt. That was one weird idea. As if a mirror'd make somebody complain!

Jeff tucked the mirror under his arm and went to the kitchen for a drink. Glancing out the window, he saw Chris ambling up the drive. Lately, Chris had been catching a later bus home. That was because he liked to sit in the cafeteria buying Cokes for two giggly girls who worked with their sister on the school paper.

"Stupid," muttered Jeff. He felt competitive, but over what he was not sure. Jeff swallowed the rest of his orange juice and went outside. He let the mirror swivel in the sunshine so that pools of light splashed over Chris's ankles.

"Neat," said Chris. "It really throws the light."

Jeff aimed reflected sun into some ornamental pines. A bird flew out with a squawk. "How far do you suppose it can send light like that?" asked Chris.

"I dunno," said Jeff. "The Navy ever send code with mirrors, you think?"

"They use signal flags, stuff like that, but I got an idea. C'mon up the hill. Let me hold it. I'll test it, see if it signals through people's windows."

"What for?" said Jeff.

"Wait and see." At the Nerones' house, Chris turned into the drive. Cara Nerone was their sister's friend, but often Chris liked to tease her. Jeff knew it was because she was the prettiest girl on the road.

Chris swung the mirror back and forth across the front of the house. The reflected sunshine slid across windows and doors.

Jeff watched from the road, then sighed. He joined Chris in the middle of the drive. He'd like to get the mirror under his bed again. It made Chris act so silly.

The Nerones' door opened. Chris slipped the mirror behind his back. "Ohhh, it's you, Chris! You too, Jeff. Whatever you're doing, go home and do it and stop bothering other people. You're blinking something right in people's eyes when they're trying to read."

Chris giggled. "Just, uh — reflecting, Cara." The

door slammed. Chris brought the mirror from behind him. "I wanted to show it to her. She'd like it — a makeup mirror, kind of."

Nettled, because the mirror was his find not Chris's to show off, Jeff wouldn't look at Chris. Instead he glanced into the mirror. Chris did too, then froze.

They both froze.

A drumroll erupted behind them, the rhythm syncopating grinds and bumps. Whooping on an off-beat came a gutsy horn, that made your hips twitchy even though the effect was, Jeff thought, real menacing. He grabbed the mirror to hold it steady because Chris's hand were shaking.

They stared into the mirror at the commotion behind them. Strutting down the drive in spiked boots and nailhead-decorated black leather were more than a dozen guys. Fantastic how they each wore an earring in one ear.

"Who're they?" whispered Chris. "Some hard-core band?"

"What are they doing *here*?" breathed Jeff. "Look at the, the, what is that stuff beside the drum and the horn?" At first he thought some of the guys held oddball guitars, but when he squinted closer, he could distinguish steel blue axe heads along one side of the "guitar" cases. Nobody made music on those instruments!

Suddenly the little hairs on the back of Jeff's neck

rose. The mirror showed him a hefty dude swinging one of those axes, swinging it his way! Jeff ducked. Something whished heavily over his head.

"Why are we standing here like a couple of patsies?" Chris groaned. "Run!"

"Which way?"

Before they could make a dash, a girl appeared in the midst of the spiky bunch. She had long dark hair, like Cara's, and wore an abbreviated leather chest protector and a sweeping denim skirt.

"Some chick!" said Chris.

"She got a horse?" Jeff spoke to Chris's ear. The girl held a chain attached to a spiked collar on the neck of a snow-white animal.

"Nah, some big old goat," murmured Chris. "Got a horn between its ears."

Eyes still glued to the mirror, Jeff said, "I don't know anything with one horn right in the middle of its forehead."

"Unicorn!" shouted Chris and whirled around. Jeff too.

The Nerones' drive stretched empty as a deserted road. On one side the iris bed waved its green spears in a gentle wind. "A unicorn is not a real animal," said Jeff.

"It's a myth from the Middle Ages or something."

"This danged mirror mixes up everything — punk rockers and myths and sexy-looking girls and *sheeee-eee*! Where are those dogs coming from?"

Staring into the scorned mirror, Jeff and Chris watched, open-mouthed, as yelping dogs surrounded the white animal. They saw the unicorn, or whatever it was, jab a hound with his horn. Blood spurted between the dog's ribs. The blood was red as a valentine. Shouting and drumming throbbed to a crescendo. "I'm leaving," whispered Jeff and sneaked a look over his shoulder . . . then relaxed. He ought to know by now there was nothing there.

Chris said, "You know, if Cara opens the door, she won't see anything, because *we* only see this weird stuff in the mirror. Here," Chris shoved the mirror at Jeff, "it's yours. I wonder who was the girl? She was cool."

"Maybe she was just, like, to get your goat, you know."

"Not funny," said Chris. "Listen, you got to get rid of that mirror. Bury it or something."

As they walked toward home, Jeff felt braver. "It would be more scientific to test it, see what else we can get to show up."

Chris wiped sweat away from his hairline. "No more, Jeff. This mirror makes fights. Suppose somebody besides us looks in this glass? Maybe they get beat up or speared before they stop looking."

Jeff grunted. "Could be. Annabel must have seen something real crazy when she was cleaning. Mom said she had a fit and left in a tizzy, and Mom — " Jeff stopped.

"See. What I said. And what about Mom?"

"Aw." Jeff grimaced.

"What about Mom?"

"In the mirror I thought she looked like a witch."

Without another word, the boys marched to their garage, and Chris lifted the lid of the nearest trash can. Jeff dropped the mirror inside.

After dinner that night, they heard a terrible racket on the street. It was a high-pitched growling from dozens of animals it seemed like. Their father stomped into the kitchen fuming about too much Thorne Center wildlife.

"What is it?" called Liz down the stairs.

"Probably raccoons getting into the garbage. They knock the lids off and scatter it all over. I put the trash by the curb for tomorrow's pickup."

"We'll fix it, Dad," said Chris. He signaled to Jeff with his eyes. They rose from the table where they'd been studying.

Outside, Chris nudged Jeff. "So how did you put that mirror in the trash?"

"Just dropped it in. You saw me."

"Sure. Mirror side *up*. Betcha."

As they approached the two cans at the gutter, chittering raccoons scuttered off in every direction.

"Take it out," said Chris. "I said we should bury it."

"I'll drop it in the pond right now," said Jeff. "Nobody cares if the fish got to fight."

MAY:
Shared Lives

ADRIENNE GILDERSLIEVE LIVED IN THE BIGGEST and the oldest house on Academy Street. Her best friend, Beth Gold, did not live on Academy Street, but she spent a lot of time there. She enjoyed the Gilderslieves' run-down Victorian house and the overgrown garden.

Adrienne and Beth had been best friends since they started first grade together. Adrienne was intelligent and wild. Beth was intelligent and compliant. It was easy to see that they needed each other.

Beth admired the fact that Adrienne could think of six other things she *had* to do, when a teacher said, "Fold your hands on your desk." Beth always did what teachers said, even though she hated herself for being such a goody-goody. On the other hand, Adrienne had pens that leaked, noisy hiccups, or even a spectacular nosebleed that had to be attended to before hands got folded.

Beth and Adrienne sometimes set each other to giggling. Over what they could never tell, but they laughed and laughed till they rolled helplessly on the playground.

It was as if, perhaps, Beth could live inside Adrienne's skin and know exactly how Adrienne felt, even though she, ordinary placid Beth Gold, could not show those feelings out in the open about herself. Beth knew how griped Adrienne was about being part of such a big family. I mean, there she was, stuck in the middle of those sisters: fifteen-year-old Barbara, who mostly lived at boarding school; next in line was Meaghan, already in junior high, then Adrienne, sort of lost before Nora, only eight; there was also a tail-ender, the four-year-old that Adrienne called the "booby-baby," Ferris.

Beth knew that Adrienne's clothes were cast-downs from Meaghan, and that she never got to throw away her own stuff because Nora inherited skirts and sweaters. She knew how frustrated Adrienne had been when she tried to teach their dog, Duchess, how to sit up and speak for a dog biscuit. Nora would come along and stick a cookie in Duchess's mouth and spoil the whole thing. Yelled at, Nora would pout and point out that the dog was partly hers, because they all shared Duchess, even Barbara, away like she was.

"Imagine owning one-fifth of a dog," protested Adrienne to her mother. But Mrs. Gilderslieve was too busy to consider the problem a problem as usual. She was on her way to work at her office downtown. She and Mr. Gilderslieve were tax consultants, and there was a nice lady, Mrs. Jacobson, who kept the household functioning every day. She was not worth complaining to. Beth understood that detail also. A housekeeper is not the same as a mother.

Still, the Gilderslieves' comfy old house had such a spate of fascinating things to play with that Beth envied Adrienne a lot. Toys and games were shared, but there were so many there was little overlap, except for the Apple II computer. It was set up in the room they called the library, and the children were allowed to use it during the day if they used it by twos, so as to help one another. Someone always had to accompany the "booby-baby" to make sure Ferris did not blow its chips or wipe out its discs, or whatever computers did when they went *kaput*. Beth and Adrienne had some pretty neat games they could play on it. When Beth began to win most of the games, Adrienne seemed to lose interest. She said computers were dull.

Instead, they went to Beth's to play with her gerbils. Frisk and Plumpkin, Adrienne said, had lively minds. Beth did not know about that, but they certainly had lively bodies. Plumpkin produced a litter, and Adrienne begged for the babies.

"When they're old enough to leave home," said Beth. "There are five, one for each of you."

"Uh-uh," said Adrienne. "They're *mine*, nobody else's."

Adrienne placed the half-grown gerbils in a glass aquarium that had once held tropical fish. Only she and Beth knew they were there on Adrienne's window seat, and the secret might have gone on forever, except for one little mistake. When Adrienne dusted her room — because all the Gilderslieves dusted their own rooms, even Ferris — she knocked the screened top off the aquarium. That was how they discovered what great jumpers gerbils can be.

Beth was visiting Adrienne the afternoon they jumped out and escaped, but it was Ferris who caught the first one. She squeezed it too tightly and got bitten on the thumb. She dropped it, and they never did find that gerbil. It seemed as if Ferris screamed for hours over "one eensy toothmark," said Adrienne, disgusted.

Unfortunately, Beth said she could not take the gerbils home again, as Adrienne's father suggested, because the daddy-gerbil would not accept the old litter. "He thinks they're strangers now," Beth said. "He'll try to kill them."

"Ma," said Adrienne, "we can't kill *children*."

"No, no we can't," said Mrs. Gilderslieve, "but we

can find them good homes." She tied the screen on the aquarium and next morning took them to the pet store on the way to her office.

"No more small animals, dear," she told Adrienne. "Nobody here is ready for such a responsibility." *I am too*, Adrienne growled. "We can't have Mrs. Jacobson chasing gerbils when she has to get dinner. No arguments, sweetie. You know how nervous arguments make me."

Adrienne told Beth during recess. Beth knew that there would always be more gerbils, but there seemed no hope of changing Mrs. Gilderslieve's mind. Beth went home with Adrienne after school to try and cheer her out of glowering glumness. Beth let Adrienne win at one of the computer games, but Adrienne said, "You let me win. That's no fun."

They went to the kitchen for milk and cookies. Mrs. Jacobson told them to help themselves. She was cleaning shelves in the old-fashioned pantry. "Never did see so many spiders!" she grumbled. "Seems like old houses attract bugs."

"That's too bad," said Beth.

Adrienne sprayed chocolate chip crumbs as she talked. "Don't think spiders are called bugs. They're different. Remember that book about the pig and Charlotte, the spider?"

Before Beth could say sure, Mrs. Jacobson screamed, "Look out!" and practically fell off the stepladder. "Biggest spider I ever saw!"

"Which way did she go?" Adrienne asked. "Big spiders are always shes." Adrienne dragged Beth into the pantry.

Beth's flesh crawled. "Kill it quick."

"No, no," said Adrienne. "I want it for my *very own*. Like in *Charlotte's Web*."

Adrienne shifted boxes and cans, and the spider zipped into the open. Beth caught her breath; it must have the leg span of a fifty-cent piece. Mrs. Jacobson, with a reflex action that would have won computer games, zapped it with a soapy sponge, *splat*.

"Awww," said Adrienne, "my pet."

"Nobody wants a spider for a pet," said Beth. "How could you ever pet a spider? Nobody ever patted that Charlotte."

Adrienne lifted the sponge. The spider was there, flat on the shelf, covered with soap suds, lifeless. The housekeeper scooped it up with a paper towel and threw it in the garbage. "Go find Nora and Ferris," she said. "Play something nice and quiet together."

"Wait," said Adrienne. She stood and looked up into the shadowy recesses near the ceiling of the pantry. "There are spider eggs, egg sacs I mean, Mrs. Jacobson. Up there."

"Thanks. I'll get to 'em," said the housekeeper.

"No, I *want* them," said Adrienne. "I need them unsoapy and unflattened. *Please*, Mrs. Jacobson."

"Ugh, you're silly," said Beth.

"But they'll hatch. Then I'll have pet spiders of

my very own," said Adrienne. She was smiling from ear to ear.

"I'll get a bag," said Beth, against her better judgment.

With the sticky eggs scooped into a brown supermarket bag, Adrienne and Beth left the kitchen.

"Where shall we put them to hatch?" Adrienne was thinking out loud.

"I suppose you want them in your room," said Beth. Her blood ran cold at the idea of anything as leggy-crawly as a spider being nearby. When she had helped scrape the egg sacs off the shelves, their very stickiness had given her the creeps.

They started up the stairs toward Adrienne's room. "I could put them in that aquarium, you know, where the gerbils were," said Adrienne.

"In that book about Charlotte," said Beth without thinking very deeply, "the new spiders let down webs and ballooned away on the wind. That's how they got to live in different places."

"Oh, yes, you're right." Adrienne stopped in the middle of the staircase. "I've got to give them more room than in some aquarium. I know how they'd feel, cramped up with too many brothers and sisters. How many do you think will hatch out? Dozens?"

"How do I know? Maybe hundreds," said Beth. She tried to get Adrienne to put the egg sacs outdoors, or at least in the garage, but Adrienne refused. She said they would not then be her pets.

"They'll be wild and not domesticated," she explained.

They settled on the library because it was light and airy and had a funny antique chandelier in the middle of the ceiling. Adrienne said the loops and wires and hanging bits of glass would make the spiders feel at home.

They scraped the egg sacs off into portions of the chandelier. They had to stand on chairs to do it. The sacs were very clingy, and it was hard work.

"I'll visit them every day," promised Adrienne. She had a dusty smudge on her freckled nose and perspiration along her hairline, but Beth could see she felt awfully good about those spider eggs.

Adrienne walked over to the silent computer. "Let's put a game on," she said. "Bombard the eggs with, uh, electrical, uh, rays . . . ?"

"I don't know if computers do that."

"Well, it'll be educational for them anyway. The hatchers, uh, hatched . . . "

"Hatchlings, maybe?"

"Yes, hatchlings. When they hatch, they'll have books" — Adrienne waved her hands at the shelves — "and encyclopedias and a computer and everything to stretch their minds."

"Adrienne, you nut!" said Beth. She flipped the computer to *on*. She hoped it would be a long long time before spiders appeared and maybe, if they were lucky, never.

Weeks passed. The weather turned quite warm, and they got out their skateboards. One Saturday afternoon everyone was coasting in the driveway, when they heard Mrs. Gilderslieve kind of yodel through the library's open windows.

"Is your mom singing?" asked Beth.

Adrienne stumbled off her skateboard, picked herself up, and said thoughtfully, "She's hollering for help, I think."

Meaghan rushed by, followed by Nora and then Ferris. "Coming Ma!"

By the time the girls got to the library, Mr. Gilderslieve was there, an arm around Mrs. Gilderslieve's shoulders. She seemed to be clutching at her head. Mr. Gilderslieve led her out of the room.

"What's wrong with Mommy?" asked Ferris.

When she looked through the library doorway, Beth could make a pretty good guess at what was bothering Mrs. Gilderslieve. She focused on a sheet of silvery strands, delicate streamers that glinted in the sunlight, dangling from the chandelier. They hung like a shifting curtain that billowed in the air from the open windows. The ends of the glittering threads held hardly visible pinpoints of baby spiders.

"They hatched!" Adrienne was jubilant. "Happy birthday, darlings."

Her father elbowed through the group. He held a can of insect spray. "Stand back, sweeties."

"Oh, no, no, no, no, no, don't kill them. They're mine!"

Meaghan had to sit on Adrienne's chest on the floor and Nora and Ferris each held a foot so Mr. Gilderslieve could spray. Beth simply held Adrienne's hand. She was sad for Adrienne, but anyone could see that thousands of baby spiders and Mrs. Gilderslieve, or anyone else, could not exist in the same room. Beth's own scalp crawled with the idea of having baby spiders making webs in her hair. Yuck!

"Okeydokey. No more bugs," said Mr. Gilderslieve and went away.

Meaghan let Adrienne sit up. A tear ran down each of Adrienne's cheeks. She wiped them off on her sleeve.

"Ugh! What do you care about a bunch of insects?" said Meaghan.

"They were *mine*," said Adrienne and sniffed.

Suddenly Beth sucked in her breath. She did not dare speak aloud, but she joggled Adrienne and pointed at the computer monitor.

Something was going on there. The glass had flicked alive, green and glowing. Slowly, pink lines slid up from the bottom and down from the top. Green lines crept in from each side. Orange circles formed in rings like ripples on a pond. Lines crossed and crisscrossed like lace.

"Huh, it's making graphics," said Meaghan, sensibly.

"Who turned it on?" asked Beth. She was ignored.

"It's making webs, *webs*, you dope," said Adrienne. "Webs," she repeated. A little smile grew on her lips.

As the monitor screen completed one circular web of threaded color, it snapped blank and began another construction of diamond crossings and intersectionings, just like webs, only green and orange and blue.

"Great, just great, Mommy is proud of you," said Adrienne.

"You're crazy," said Meaghan. "Some dumb dead spiders can't make a computer spin webs. I mean that's really loony."

"They could too. They are. They're *haunting* it," said Adrienne.

"They're *ghosts*?" said Ferris. She began to suck her thumb.

"Of course not," said Mrs. Gilderslieve. She appeared in a terry cloth bathrobe, a large towel turbaning her hair. "I'm sure Daddy got rid of the insects."

The latest pink and green and orange webbing faded to a dot on the screen. In its place, running fresh across the monitor, came letters . . . words . . . a sentence . . . two sentences.

"We are not insects. We are arachnids."

Adrienne chortled, choked, and rolled with glee

on the carpet. Mrs. Gilderslieve gasped.

"What are ar-ar-arachnids?" asked Nora.

"Spiders," said Mrs. Gilderslieve in a small voice.

"I want Daddy," said Ferris and ran.

Everyone followed, leaving Beth and Adrienne in the library.

"Shouldn't we turn the computer off?" whispered Beth.

"They'll do it when they're ready," said Adrienne, arms folded on her chest.

"I'm going," said Beth. "It's too spooky." She yanked at Adrienne to get her to move, but Adrienne refused and beamed toward the computer.

Flip — there came another message rippling across the screen, a brief command. Beth shuddered. It read, "Send flies."

JUNE:
The Barbecue

EVERY JUNE THE ACADEMY STREET CROWD HAD
an end-of-school barbecue. This year it was in the
Gilderslieves' backyard. The date was set for the
twenty-third, and Adrienne's mother made sure
every boy and girl on the street received an invita-
tion, even big Jesse Kujak.

"Wellll, I guess he has to come because he lives
here," said Adrienne, "and Beth has to come even if
she doesn't live here, okay?"

"She practically does, doesn't she?" her mother
said. "And how about that little girl who visits her
grandmother? I see her walking up the hill on
Saturdays."

"Lucy? Sure, okay. She's in my class. Can we each

have three hamburgers and gallons of Kool-Aid?"

On the twenty-third, the weather was perfect. Duchess wakened at sunup, and nosed open her dog-door from the laundry room. Jumping outside, she shook herself till her ears rattled. She breathed deeply of fresh air. And sneezed. Then showed her teeth in incipient anxiety. There was a layer of something unfamiliar that tickled at her nose. Even her hackles rose. A dog could never be sure: If something was unfamiliar, it might also be a menace. Duchess pushed through the unlatched front gate. Best to give Academy Street an early A.M. checkout.

"Grrr." The rumble started deep in her throat. A tall jogger was coming down the hill, and she had not been aware of his going up. Ordinarily, even if inside, Duchess knew when people or dogs or cats walked on Academy Street. How had she missed him? Huff, she was slipping, that's what, getting on in years.

As the jogger drew nearer, Duchess saw he had long hair that flapped on his shoulders and blew across his eyes. No male on Academy Street had long hair like that. Again, Duchess showed her teeth. The jogger was wearing a sweat suit, but he was not sweating. Coolness seemed to surround him like a bubble, and his running was effortless. He was tall and bony, and his feet, which were bare and bony, hardly touched the pavement. He wore a sweatband around his hair, but, if you could believe, it had a

glowing jewel in the middle of it. Kind of a —
grrr — third eye. It flashed at Duchess, and she began to pant. Slung by one strap over a shoulder was
a knapsack of such brilliant stuff that Duchess
blinked as the golden reflections momentarily
blinded her.

"Gr-wuff," she meant to say. Her mouth opened
wide, but nothing came out. The jogger floated by
with a grin and a sparkle. Duchess closed in and
aimed a bite at those bare ankles. Missed.

Duchess put on a burst of speed and snapped
again. At thin air. The jogger, without stopping,
reached a hand into a pocket and scattered bits and
pieces of what looked like flower petals behind him.
One landed on Duchess's nose, and she licked it off.
Yum! Better than roast beef. She lapped up several
bits and then followed the jogger and his flying hair
around the corner of Academy Street and onto Pond
Road. When he stopped at Prince Street, she stopped
too. "Excellent beast," said the jogger. Duchess
wagged her tail.

A green truck was coming down Prince Street.
The jogger waved at it. The truck drew up and
paused. It was full of rakes and lawn mowing equip-
ment. Duchess knew its smell because it brought a
gardener to Academy Street. The jogger got in and
the truck departed.

Duchess had been sitting and panting heavily.
Now she got up and shook herself. Wait a minute

. . . what was that delicious smell from where the jogger had stood? There was a small folded paper bag left on the gravel. He must have dropped his lunch. Carefully Duchess took the brown paper in her mouth and, drooling a bit, carried home a reek of hot dog.

She dropped it on her kitchen dog bed. It smelled great. Duchess might have torn open the bag then and there, except that Mrs. Jacobson had arrived early to make barbecue preparations, and she noticed Duchess. "Don't need you underfoot today," she said. "I'm too busy. Shoo. Skedaddle." She waved a broom at Duchess, who left the bag and retreated outside to flop in the sunshine. Doggedly, Duchess felt it was hard to be so unappreciated.

Late in the afternoon, everyone gathered for the barbecue. The perfect weather of the morning had added a little teasing breeze. The paper napkins, piled up by Mrs. Jacobson, flopped onto the grass, and empty plastic cups tumbled about. Nora went back and forth to pick them up.

Mr. Gilderslieve was in charge of the hamburgers. "Don't touch that grill," he said to Adrienne, who was hovering close to the fire.

"Dad," said Adrienne, "the hamburgers are flip-flopping all by themselves. See?" A hamburger lifted at least an inch into the air and fell back. Sparks flew.

"Nonsense," said her father. "They're broiling nicely. Help bring out the rest of the picnic."

Jesse carried out the five gallon punch jug with a spigot on the bottom. The really funny thing was that you did not have to turn the handle of the spigot to get a drink. Beth discovered it first thing, when she held her cup under the little faucet. As long as you held a cup under it, punch flowed; when she moved her cup to the side, the flow stopped. "Oh, my," said Beth. She did not mention it to anyone. She stood beside the jug for a while waiting to see if anyone else discovered how amazing it was.

While she lingered, sipping a little now and then, Jesse brought three cups; one for himself, one for Liz, and one for Meaghan. He too found out that he did not have to turn the spigot OFF between cups.

"Hey," he said to Beth, "you see that? Some smarty machine." He filled a dozen cups. He left them on the table for others. Shaking his head, he went off with three. "Must be a computerized thermos. I didn't know they could do that."

Jesse tried to compliment Mrs. Gilderslieve about the jug, but she was terribly distracted by a kitchen mix-up. Mrs. Jacobson, who had of course gone home, had made a mistake in the barbecue menu. She'd baked a big pot of hot chili, instead of franks and beans. Ferris insisted on a hot dog, and there weren't any.

Presented with a hamburger on a bun like everyone else, Ferris dashed it to the lawn and started to wail.

Like a banshee, thought Beth.

Mrs. Gilderslieve put her hands over her ears, but Nora grinned. "Ferris can holler louder than anybody," she said.

From where she crouched under the redwood picnic table, Duchess said to a large toad hidden in the grass beside her, "I'll have to give that child the snack I found."

Duchess trotted into the open kitchen. She reappeared with the jogger's paper bag in her mouth. Duchess said as she dropped the bag at Ferris's feet, "*Bon appétit*, little one." Nobody understood her to utter anything but a whiny growl.

Duchess lipped up Ferris's dropped hamburger and crawled under the table again to share it with the toad. There was a lot of racket going on around Ferris, about where Duchess had found a hot dog and whether Mrs. Gilderslieve would allow Ferris to eat it.

Duchess ignored the ruckus. "Better than flies, eh?" she said to her friend.

After a surfeit of hamburgers and chili, Nora was sent for the bags of marshmallows and a dozen toasting forks. Mr. Gilderslieve lifted the rack away from the hot coals so that everyone could hold a marshmallow close to the heat.

Whoosh! Flames engulfed each marshmallow before it could toast. The second that anyone, even Mr. G., put a fork of marshmallow near the glow, the white burst into a torch. Before long, everyone stood and whirled a flaming marshmallow overhead. The party looked like a torchbearers' parade, thought Beth.

Then she noticed Lucy was actually eating hers. As soon as Lucy placed a hand near her burning forkful, the flames extinguished themselves. Gingerly, Beth did the same. As she peeled away the black, Lucy stopped her.

"No, no," said Lucy, "the black is most delicious of all. See, the marshmallow isn't even too hot, and every part tastes awfully good."

While Mr. and Mrs. Gilderslieve said over and over, "Careful, careful," everyone ate unbelievable marshmallows, crisp on the outside and melted soft within. Even Cara, who was so fastidious, got sticky. Ferris managed to get goo in her hair but was very quiet about it.

"It's Midsummer Night's Eve," said Beth suddenly.

"What-what?" said Jesse.

"Things are supposed to happen on Midsummer Night's Eve," said Beth. "That's what people used to believe. You built bonfires for the fairies and banshees. I mean, people did in olden times."

"How do you know about such things?" asked Jeff Pennell.

"Beth knows everything," said Adrienne, " 'cause she reads everything."

"It's the longest day, the shortest night," said Beth. "The sun stays still, and there are spirits in the wind."

"I think I hear them," said Linda. She giggled, then sighed.

"And even the animals are supposed to talk."

"Sometimes in the middle of winter, too," muttered Streak Baxter.

"What-what?" said Jesse, who was standing close beside him.

"Nothing," said Streak and turned away. Jesse grabbed his elbow tight as tight.

"Uh, well, it's just an idea, maybe animals talk only we don't understand what they say, only if we concentrate, sort of, or something kind of opens our ears . . . "

Something opens our ears. Jesse's flesh shuddered. Streak was a good friend, but Jesse had never told anyone about those crazy sneakers. Jesse cleared his throat and said, "Imagination does real pe-cool-yar stuff, I betcha," but Streak had gone to toast another marshmallow.

"Better put the floodlights on," said Mr. Gilderslieve. "Longest day or not, it's getting too dark, I think."

"Please, not yet," said Adrienne. "The dark is *special* tonight, Dad, and we like it a little spooky on our street. Spooky is good? Isn't it?" She looked around the group. Everyone stood close together now. One by one, they nodded, rather solemn, even Ferris, who slipped her hand into Beth's and said nothing for a change.

Little blue flames danced over the top of the open barbecue, and a whiff of smoke reminded Lucy of the smell from Gramps's old Singer. As the air swirled the smoke in higher and higher spirals, Ferris whispered to Beth, "Am I scared?"

Soothingly, Beth squeezed Ferris's hand, then suddenly, not reassuring at all, yelped, "What's *that*?" and pointed. A sparkled waver of brilliance glinted beneath a dark spruce. It seemed three-dimensional, almost solid, blinding and bright.

"Gold! Money bags," said Jeff Pennell. The breeze ruffled the branches together in a chuckle of sound.

"Not money," said Lucy. "I think it's someone carrying a golden flag."

"Oh, poo," said Cara, "it's only a spiderweb where the last sun shines on it."

"Great! A golden spiderweb!" shouted Adrienne. Ferris put the thumb of her other hand in her mouth.

"Now it's gone," said Linda. "The sun's set." For some dumb reason, she felt close to tears.

Under the table, Duchess observed, "That jogger's

knapsack sparkled the same way. I hope he wasn't here hunting for his lunch."

"Wise up, Duchess," said the toad. "Got to expect a little Manifestation on this Night, right?"

"Huff?" said Duchess. "Manifestation? Oh. I see. You mean the Academy Street jogger comes at Midsummer? Right."

"Jogger, or Visitor, or Lord of the Dance. Or whatever." Toad belched, "Kkk-kroke," and breathed deeply with a swell of his white throat. "Been nice talking with you, neighbor." Then he hopped fatly away.